The man who had caused Sara so much mental anguish stood on the windswept cliff in front of her

"You are Ransom Shepard," she proclaimed hoarsely. It came out sounding like an accusation, as though she'd said, "You are *slime.*"

He appeared curious, then nodded.

"Ooh!" Sara swung out blindly, smacking him across a lean cheek. "I'll see you in prison!" she cried, venting all the rage she'd carried around with her since her younger sister's disappearance.

Ransom took a step backward and appeared about to speak, although he didn't seem particularly troubled by her attack. No doubt having women slap his face was an everyday experience for him.

Once more Sara's fury overcame her, and she flung out her arm to strike his face again. "How dare you lure away an innocent girl to be your mail-order bride!"

Ransom caught her wrist in a strong grip and said, "So, your visit concerns our little Lynn."

Dear Reader,

A Bride for Ransom is my twelfth romance novel, but it's special to me because it's the first time I've been able to actually attend my hero and heroine's wedding. I know we all finish a book we particularly like, with characters we've grown to love, and we imagine what their wedding will be like. What a pleasurable fantasy! Well, we authors are no different. So, when I was asked to be a part of the Bridal Collection, I was thrilled. A wedding, at last!

I'd already become enthralled by my chosen locale—the Pribilof Islands in the Bering Sea. Part of Alaska, these tiny islands suited my purpose, because I needed a remote setting—a place from which a reluctant heroine could not easily escape. Unfortunately, even the remote Pribilofs have a perfectly wonderful telephone system (which works most of the time), and plenty of planes in and out, so I had to create an extra island—one slightly more remote and vastly less accessible.

Though St. Catherine Island doesn't exist, everything you discover about it holds true for the real islands, St. Paul and St. George. The Pribilof Islands are a fascinating place, with strong, friendly people and a rich Aleut heritage. I would be horribly remiss if I didn't express my deepest thanks to one person, in particular, on St. Paul Island. I was a stranger who called one day, out of the blue, asking if anyone would answer questions for me. He was a busy man with great responsibilities, but he gave selflessly of his time on numerous occasions. Because of his love for his land and his people, he assisted me in making *A Bride for Ransom* a story I'm proud of. Though my Pribilovian colleague is too modest to accept public accolades, he is a man to whom I will always be grateful.

So, thanks, fella!

I hope you all enjoy my story and this glimpse into a proud but little-known American culture. I also hope you fall in love with my hero and heroine, as I did, and thrill, as I did, when their wedding vows are exchanged in a truly unique and Pribilovian wedding.

Sincerely,

Renee Roszel

A BRIDE FOR RANSOM

Renee Roszel

Harlequin Books

TORONTO • NEW YORK • LONDON
AMSTERDAM • PARIS • SYDNEY • HAMBURG
STOCKHOLM • ATHENS • TOKYO • MILAN
MADRID • WARSAW • BUDAPEST • AUCKLAND

To my sons, Doug and Randy
(Heroes-In-Training)

ISBN 0-373-03251-X

Harlequin Romance first edition February 1993

A BRIDE FOR RANSOM

Printed in U.S.A.

CHAPTER ONE

THE MAN WHO HAD CAUSED Sara so much mental anguish was barely one hundred yards ahead. Broad-shouldered, wearing a green turtleneck sweater, he was standing on the edge of a cliff facing the sea. It tested her mightily to see this... this *cradle robber* so at ease! What kind of man *was* he? What kind of man would lure away an awkward, naive sixteen-year-old girl to be his mail-order bride?

Sara promised herself she would be calm and rational when she confronted the man who'd prompted her sister to run away from home. But her week-long state of near hysteria made remaining composed a monumental task. Of course Sara was furious with her sister, Lynn, for packing up and sneaking off as she had. Lynn was more like a daughter to Sara than a sister, since Sara had raised her from the time she was eight. She prayed that her sister—such an innocent when it came to men and their passions—was safe and well. Her first order of business, when she finally saw Lynn again, was to hug the stuffing out of her; then she planned to wring her freckled little neck!

Sara's fears had ebbed slightly on the last leg of her long journey from Kansas to this remote island in the Bering Sea. The crusty old pilot who'd flown her from the larger St. Paul Island to this tiny dot on the ocean had heard of this...this conniving, underhanded Ransom Shepard. Sara realized she was prejudging the man, but fatigue and anguish had pushed her well beyond social niceties. To be fair, the tobacco-chewing pilot had described Mr. Shepard simply as a bird-watcher—not as a corrupter of innocents.

Sara had formed a picture of him in her mind: bespectacled, bandy-legged, dreary. Exactly the type who might have to send away for a mail-order bride. That had eased her torment—momentarily. But when she was directed to this remote corner of St. Catherine Island, she'd been told that Ranson Shepard owned the whole peninsula. And the hulking brute ahead of her in thigh-hugging jeans was no bandy-legged, bespectacled birder!

He was big, over six feet tall with a muscular physique and long, corded legs. The kind of man who could lift a truck if he felt an urge to. She clutched the handle of her overnight case almost desperately, feeling her hard-won control sliding even further. Something in the pit of her stomach told her this was not the sort of man who would order up a bride by mail and then care that she was a starry-eyed runaway looking for adventure or a mere high school girl. He looked like a man who took what he wanted when he wanted it, without regard for the consequences. Sara had an unattractive urge to tear him limb from limb, which wouldn't be all that easy, considering the fact that she was five foot five and probably about half his weight.

By the time she reached the rugged cliff and was nearing the stranger who had taken advantage of her sister's innocence, she was struggling to rein in her temper. Even though she was a redhead, Sara prided herself on being cool and logical rather than fiery and irrational. Still, the intense emotions she'd kept bottled up for nine horrible days were now at explosive levels, and unfortunately Ransom Shepard just might bear witness to an unprecedented eruption of temper. She struggled to keep her anger and panic in check; she gritted her teeth, clamped her jaws and marched steadfastly along. As she marched, she repeated a warning to herself: *Give him a chance to explain. Give him a chance to explain. Give him*. . .

Caught up in her mental turmoil, she paid scant heed to the salt air that wafted upward from the sea, the symphony of seabirds diving and fluttering overhead, or the shy purple and red wildflowers that kissed the cuffs of her jeans. She advanced determinedly, her blood pounding in her ears, her eyes fastened on the scoundrel—*No, no, don't think that!* she admonished herself—the *person* with the powerful shoulders and widely braced legs.

Nor did she take much notice of the charcoal-colored beach far below, where seals shuffled about on rubbery flippers. She was wholly intent on keeping herself from jumping on this mountain of a man, clawing and scratching for all her worth.

The rush of the sea breeze and the cacophony of darting birds had masked her approach. But when she was a few steps from the stranger, he seemed to sense her and turned. Dusky curls drifted across his broad brow. His expression was closed, as though he was deep in thought or perturbed in some way.

As she moved closer, something in her found it necessary to record his uncommonly good looks. His deep-set eyes were dark gray, like the beaches of his island. Glistening like antique pewter, they seemed knowing, sharply assessing, yet remote. And his nose was far from the beakish protrusion she'd envisioned. It was a straight nose, rather noble as noses go. But his mouth was what drew her gaze. Even set in a grim line, it was a masterpiece of masculinity, with lips that were neither too wide nor too full. A man's mouth. A mouth made for kissing. She cringed at the thought of her impressionable sister confronted by such masculine perfection.

Her emotions had swung from sheer dread to murderous violence when she'd discovered where Lynn had gone—to a bridegroom in the wilds of Alaska's Pribilof Islands. She'd had to spend every dime she'd saved to get up here to the ends of the earth. The money had been a nest egg, so that one day Lynn could better herself by going to nursing college. But now, having seen the gorgeous stranger her sister was dealing with, Sara feared poor Lynn's virtue was long past saving.

He was so handsome! So horribly handsome! What appalling flaw did he have that he couldn't find a willing bride nearby? Why had he been forced to advertise for a wife? With this new dread slicing through her frayed emotions, her temper was cut free of its tenuous link to etiquette, and she found herself proclaiming hoarsely, "You are Ransom Shepard." It came out sounding like an accusation, as though she'd said, "You are *slime!*"

He appeared curious, then nodded.

"Ooh!" she howled. Dropping her overnight case, she swung out blindly, smacking him across a lean cheek. "I'll see you in prison!" she cried, venting all the rage she'd carried around with her since Lynn had disappeared. Somewhere a little voice was reminding her that Lynn was partly at fault, but Lynn wasn't here. Besides, Lynn was only sixteen. This man was in his midthirties. He was entirely too old—and too...too something! He looked like a man of great experience where women were concerned, and this fact made Sara even more frightened for her sister's welfare.

He took a step backward and appeared about to speak. His eyes narrowed, but he didn't seem particularly troubled by her attack. No doubt having a woman slap his face was an everyday experience for him. And the reasons he was accustomed to being slapped were doubtlessly why a man with such riveting physical presence had found it necessary to order his bride by mail. Once more Sara's fury overcame her, and she drew back her arm to strike his face again.

This time she found her wrist caught in a strong grip as he cautioned, "Only one free slap to a customer, miss. Before you hit me a second time, I plan to deserve it."

She yanked at his hold, protesting, "Start planning, buster! You'll serve hard time for this, you low-crawling toad!"

That remark seemed to give him pause and his eyes widened a bit. Releasing her arm, he said, "Most women don't feel that strongly about men touching their wrists." One corner of his mouth lifted skeptically. "You must be fun on a date."

His nonchalance about the whole matter added fuel to the inferno of Sara's anger. She pulled herself up to her full height, crying, "Have you no shame? Do you think luring away an innocent sixteen-year-old girl for...for *carnal* purposes is something to joke about?"

There was the briefest moment when Sara thought his face registered surprise, but too quickly his expression changed back to the same grim one she'd seen when he'd first turned around. "So," he began, crossing his arms over his wide chest. "Your visit concerns our little Lynn."

She matched his stance, crossed arms for crossed arms. Somehow she didn't feel all that secure in her defiant posture. Nonetheless, with staunch bravado, she challenged, "My visit concerns *my* little Lynn, and to see you behind bars, you...you..."

"Low-crawling toad?" he said helpfully.

Sara blinked, fighting sudden tears. "I'm glad you think this is so funny!"

"Look," he said, wearily, "you're clearly overwrought, so I won't take offense—"

"Take all the offense you want," she fairly hissed.

As she cut across his attempt at appeasement, he clamped his jaws together as if trying to control his own temper.

All Sara's plans to give this man a chance to explain were trampled beneath her burgeoning fear and distrust. She knew she was overreacting, but she couldn't help herself. Lynn was the only family she had left. She'd lost both her mother and father in a car accident when she was seventeen, and for the past week she'd been plagued with terror that she might have lost Lynn, too. Working to keep from visibly trembling, she cried, "What have you done with Lynn Eller?"

"I have no idea where she is," he remarked coolly.

Sara's lips opened in shock. She'd never figured on this. St. Catherine Island was only twenty-two square miles of untamed tundra, alive with arctic foxes, reindeer and seabirds. There weren't many places Lynn could have fled. "Did she run away? What did you do to her?" Sara asked in a frightened whisper. "If she's hurt I'll—"

"I know." He nodded, frowning. "You'll have me behind bars. This is where I came in." Cocking his head, he indicated the beach below. "She went walking. She said she'd be back more than an hour ago. Apparently she changed her mind."

Sara peered over the cliff. The beach glistened like a narrow carpet of black pearls as the cobalt water lapped across its surface. "Well... well, go look for her! Didn't it occur to you she might have drowned?" she demanded her voice anguished.

He turned to face the sea. "No one in his right mind would get near the water. As you've probably noticed, the temperature is forty degrees. But I admit," he added, sounding slightly annoyed, "I wouldn't put much past that little piece of work. Taggart's with her, though. He's a good swimmer."

"Taggart?" she twisted around to stare at him, her temper surging. "Oh, my dear Lord. She's your bride, yet you've allowed her to go off alone with another man!"

One brow arched dubiously as he peered at her. "Miss whatever-your-name-is, you have quite a dirty mind. Taggart happens to be my fourteen-year-old—"

"I don't want the details!" she ranted on. "This whole mail-order-bride thing is so upset—" She halted, finally registering what he'd said. "Your fourteen-year-old what?"

His mouth twitched, exhibiting amused contempt. "Son," he stated curtly. "I admit Tag's no angel, but I don't think he'd violate Lynn." His glance sharp and inquisitive, he added, "Now I seem to be at a disadvantage here. You know who I am, but I can only imagine that you're either a relative of Lynn's or possibly her parole officer?"

His wry tone irked Sara, and she blurted hotly, "Eller! Sara Eller—*Miss* Eller to you. I'm Lynn's sister. And her guardian, I might add. Don't change the subject."

"Forgive me, *Miss* Eller." His gaze ranged over her, assessing what he saw. She had the uncomfortable feeling he found her lacking, especially when he said, "There are those who might say you're not doing a very good job as Lynn's guardian at the moment."

His words felt like a slap, though the reprimand had been softly spoken. It was true, no matter how painful it was to hear. She hadn't been an effective guardian to Lynn. But then, she'd been little more than a child herself when she'd taken over Lynn's care. She supposed she should have disciplined her sister more, not put up with so much back talk. But she'd loved her; Lynn was all she had. Sara might have made mistakes, but she'd done the best she could.

Pride stiffening her spine, she shot back, "How dare you? You, who would entice an underage girl away from her home with promises of marriage to a wealthy man and an easy life on an island paradise. How dare you find fault with me!"

"Your sister came here of her own free will. Beyond that, she told me she had no home, no family. Where would *you* place blame, Miss Eller?" he challenged gently.

She swallowed hard, feeling as though she'd been stabbed. Lynn couldn't have dismissed her so completely after all the years Sara had worked and scrimped to keep a roof over their heads. Maybe she'd been overprotective, but not to the extent that Lynn would do something this rash. Refusing to believe such a thing about the sister she loved more than her own life, she cried, "Liar! She wouldn't have said that!"

His lean face darkened, growing more forbidding. Without comment, he looked toward the somber sky. "It's going to rain, Miss Eller. Would you care to continue my character assassination inside?"

"I wouldn't set foot inside your den of iniquity if the hounds of hell were nipping at my heels! Find Lynn, and we'll be on our way."

He eyed her speculatively. "On your way where?"

"Why, back to that dilapidated excuse for an airplane and on to St. Paul, then to the first available connecting flight to Anchorage and Kansas, of course."

His chuckle was contemptuous. "That dilapidated excuse for an airplane is long gone. What do you think St. Catherine's air strip is—LAX?"

"What are you talking about?" she breathed, an odd helplessness enveloping her.

He pursed his lips, and his silence had begun to infuriate her before he finally explained. "I fear the hounds of hell are going to get in some good nibbles before you catch that connecting flight. Old Krukoff only makes a trip to St. Catherine on Wednesdays, to bring in supplies and transport the occasional visitor. Barring bad weather, he should be back in a week."

"A week?" Sara echoed, incredulous.

"Or longer, if the plane breaks down," he amended. "That happens every couple of—"

"What are you, some kind of sadist?" Sara was sure he was goading her with this catalog of potential calamities. "I bet it thrills you to pieces to see women suffer!"

His gray eyes flashed. "I've had better thrills," he informed her, his tone colored by disgust.

Wincing at his rebuke, she spun away from him, her thoughts churning. What was she to do? She was going to have to spend the next week on this tiny island—all too near this distressing man! She had little money for lodging, though what she'd seen of the island didn't leave her optimistic of finding any. She'd seen nothing that resembled a hotel. There'd been a church and a cluster of cottages around a modest harbor. Still, maybe there was a small inn. A small cheap inn. She clung to that hope.

Calling up her waning courage, she retorted, "Well, I see no point in discussing this further. Just direct me to the nearest guest house."

He didn't answer her until she had unwillingly faced him. She knew he was being manipulative, but she couldn't help lifting her eyes to meet his. His expression was impassive, but his gaze sparkled with mirth at her expense. "Would you prefer a beachfront condo?" he inquired, "Or perhaps the penthouse of the St. Catherine Hilton?"

Renewed foreboding crept up her spine. "Are you saying there are no hotels on this island?"

"Notice any nipping from those hellhounds yet?"

She felt stung by his sarcasm and to hide her turmoil tossed him a haughty glance. "Surely someone could put us up."

His perusal continued to be direct and disconcerting, telling her he could put her up if he chose to. The message was so unsubtle she blurted, "I'd rather shoot myself in the foot than endure your hospitality."

"I haven't offered you my hospitality, Miss Eller," he reminded her with a slow half grin.

Taken aback, she glared at him. "Well, then, where would you suggest I *go?*"

When his brows lifted expressively, she realized she'd left herself wide open for a variety of insults. But all he said was, "It's not a very big island, Miss Eller. Most of the village folks live modest lives and have no excess of either space or food."

"We can stay in the church!" she declared.

"It's one large room, Miss Eller, and it's open to villagers twenty-four hours a day. You might find that less than satisfactory at times."

At a loss, Sara floundered about for a solution. After several false starts, she gave up, deciding to be brutally direct. "I couldn't stay with you, Mr. Shepard. And I must remove Lynn from your...authority. It's clear that you have some, er, character flaw that requires you to engage your female companionship by mail. I assure you, I don't care to be in close enough contact with you to discover what that flaw might be."

For a long moment, he stared at her, his jaw working. His silence and unwavering gaze were unnerving. At odds with her desire to do so, she found herself curious about what possible defect this man might have. Did he kick puppies and spit tobacco on the floor? Whatever the blot on his character, it certainly wasn't evident in his looks.

After a tense minute, an ironic smile tugged at the corners of his mouth. "In defense of those who order their brides by mail," he said, "have you considered the fact that there are simply more men in the Alaskan wilds than there are women?" His expression became increasingly rueful as he added, "It might be exactly the avenue for a sharp-tongued spitfire such as yourself to snag a not-too-choosy mate."

She gasped, mortification heating her cheeks. "Why you... I—I'm not a sharp-tongued spitfire!"

"No?" He appeared skeptical, almost amused. "You slap me, then call me a low-crawling worm—"

"Toad!" she corrected defiantly.

"This may startle you, Miss Eller, but being called a toad is not viewed as an endearment by most men."

A raindrop pelted Sara in the eye, and she flinched. In the next few seconds the clouds were spitting fat drops all about them. In a futile gesture to ward off the coming storm, she lifted her hands above her head, looking at Ransom Shepard with distress. He was right of course. She'd acted abominably. With less rancor, she sputtered, "Well, uh, 'toad' may have been a bit strong, but look at it from my side. My sister's only sixteen, and you're...why, you've got a son almost as old as Lynn. For a week I've been sick with worry about her! How would you have expected me to act?"

His features grew less harsh. "I understand." And with a brief nod toward his home, he offered, "We really should go inside."

She shook her head. "No, thank you. I'd rather not—"

"I'm no happier about this than you. But I do have room, and I'm partly responsible for your being here. Besides, your sister's already staying with me. Remember?"

This prompting made her anger return with a vengeance. Pinning him with a hostile glare, she opened her mouth, bent on rejecting his offer, and was startled to discover she couldn't find her voice. His silver eyes held an unexpected hypnotic quality. Fighting a crazy desire to be drawn into his gaze, she stared mutely off into the distance. A solid-looking house loomed ahead of them. Blunt and square, it had cement walls that were hidden by overlapping wood shingles—a style, Sara had noticed, peculiar to the Pribilof Islands. The structure's shingles were gray and unpainted. All in all, it was a humble dwelling devoid of architectural excesses.

An enclosed covered porch jutted from the nearest wall, its door standing open. The house appeared both strong and sheltering, and it emanated an oddly welcoming yet forbidding appeal—like the man who resided there. She chewed the inside of her cheek, knowing she had to seek refuge with him, but not wanting to. There was something... unorthodox about this man. Something brooding and unpredictable that made her apprehensive.

At her continued silence, he said, "For the record, I don't coerce women to stay in my home against their will—or to sleep in my bed."

His remark brought back a vivid reminder of Lynn's predicament. Knowing her sister as she did—a book-smart pudgy dreamer who'd never dated, with schoolgirl notions of love and princes on white chargers—she worried that this attractive, soft-spoken man would have had to say very little to "coerce" Lynn into his bed.

Sara felt a shaft of dismay. For the first time, she fully understood what she'd refused to face when Ransom Shepard turned around and she'd been struck by his bold good looks. She understood why she'd been absolutely blinded with rage. It wasn't because Lynn had left Kansas for him. No, seeing him in the flesh, so powerfully handsome, the truth had hit her like a ton of bricks. The choice Lynn had made was irrevocable by now. Surely with this man's seduction, Lynn was lost to her forever, and Sara was alone. Impressionable Lynn could never have resisted this man, no matter what his flaws. Feeling beaten, she warned almost pleadingly, "If you've damaged my sister in any way, I'll—"

He grabbed her overnight case and took her arms, pivoting her away from the cliff. "It's raining, Miss Eller. If you stand here in that thin jacket much longer, you'll catch pneumonia. Why don't we go inside and wait for your allegedly damaged sister?" He glanced sidelong at Sara, catching her hesitant gaze. "She does have the sense to come in out of the rain, doesn't she?"

Inside her head, a bothersome voice asked, *Just how much sense* does *Lynn have to get you both involved in such a terrible mess?* But Sara had too much family pride to voice her doubts about her sister's rash behavior, especially to this man. Smarting from his censure, she tried to jerk free of his hold, but failed. Without much choice, she was pulled along beside him. He was right about one thing at least. Her windbreaker and cotton sweater weren't much protection from the rain. Feeling thwarted and still fretting over her sister's well-being, she demanded, "Are you two married?"

He cast her a brief caustic glance, but said nothing.

"Are you?" They'd reached the cement steps, their footsteps echoing dully as they ran for the shelter of the porch. Fearing his answer, she rushed on, "I may not be Lynn's lawful guardian—I mean, we never did anything *legal* after Mom and Dad died—but I talked to a Kansas legal-aid lawyer before I came up here, and she said, being underage, Lynn'd have to petition the court for approval of the marriage or something like that. She hasn't had time to do that, has she? *Has she?* Are you two *legally* married?"

"What do you think?" he growled, upsetting her further.

At the door, she was finally able to yank her arm free, and she whirled to face him. "This is no time for guessing games!"

Turning the knob, he motioned for her to enter. When she merely stood glowering, he shook his head and sighed. "No. We're not married. Does that put your mind at rest?"

"Sis?" came a distant querulous voice. Sara jerked toward the sound and saw Lynn, who was shorter and stouter than her, stumbling to a halt several feet from the porch. "Sara? Is that you?" This time the voice sounded strained with anxiety.

Someone else had been running toward the porch, too. A gangling dark-haired boy, taller than Lynn. They were both clad in jeans and parkas. His was blue. Sara recognized Lynn's yellow one—bought last fall and already too short in the arms. Both teens were soaked, and their sneakers were mud-caked.

"It would seem she's still living," Ransom ventured dryly.

"Uh-oh," Lynn groaned, beginning to back away.

"Lynn!" Sara cried, thankful to see her sister alive and well. Rushing down the steps, she grabbed her by both wrists. "Lynn, baby!" Tears came flooding in her eyes, and her voice trembled with relief. "You gave me the scare of my life! I ought to strangle you!"

Feeling Lynn's arms go stiff as the girl attempted to pull away, Sara subsided and simply dragged her into the protection of the porch. The boy bounded up after them.

Once again facing her sister, Sara inspected her despairingly. But she found herself unable to shout or scold, her relief making her forgive everything. A reluctant smile tugged at her lips, new tears blurring her vision as she hugged Lynn hard, whispering, "Thank goodness you're safe!"

Holding her runaway sister slighty away, Sara took another appraising look. Lynn's hair hung to just below her shoulders in dripping disarray. Though they were both redheads, Sara had been blessed with thick, dark mahogany tresses while Lynn's hair had always been limp, thin and carrot orange. Lynn's hazel eyes, the only physical characteristic the two shared exactly, were wide with apprehension. Rivulets of rain trickled down her freckle-strewn face, but otherwise she looked healthy. It took great effort but Sara was able to control her voice and ask, "Lynn, are you all right? Has that man hurt you in any way?"

Lynn appeared confused. "What man?"

Unable to believe her sister's thickheadedness in the face of everything that had happened, she motioned toward Ransom. "*This* man—the one who advertised for a bride. I finally found that Alaskan magazine with the ads in it. How could you have run off like that? How could you have stolen the charge card I keep in the closet for emergencies—and forged my name?" In her anxiety, Sara tightened her hold on Lynn's arm. "The only way I could find you was by calling the credit-card company after I'd discovered that the card was gone. They told me about the airline tickets you'd charged—to Anchorage and St. Catherine. Why..."

Sara was so upset, she couldn't trust her voice to go on. She didn't want to burst into tears in front of this objectionable stranger, but her emotions were warring between fierce anger at Lynn's irresponsible behavior and sob-filled relief that she was okay. She bit her lower lip to keep it from quivering.

"Tag," Ransom said, "why don't we leave these ladies alone for a minute." With a nod, he indicated for the dark-haired youth to precede him into the house. The boy looked somewhat like his father, Sara noticed vaguely, though he had no slashing cleft in his chin, and his eyes were a vivid green. Tag shrugged and did as requested, leaving Sara standing alone with her contrary sister.

Once she heard the door to the house click shut, Sara murmured brokenly, "Has he . . . hurt you?"

Lynn squinted, making a face. She seemed both mystified and cautious. "Who?"

"Ransom Shepard!" Sara hissed the name, shocked at the vehemence in her voice.

"Rance?" Lynn asked incredulously. "Why would he hurt me? He's a happenin' dude."

Sara looked heavenward. "Spare me the slang. Has he laid, er, a hand on you? I mean, he hasn't tried to . . . to kiss you or . . . anything?"

Lynn's eyes widened with realization. "Oh! That!"

"Yes, that," Sara repeated, dreading the worst.

She was startled when Lynn giggled and said, "It's a funny story, really."

"I'd kill for a good laugh right now, Lynn," Sara said through gritted teeth. "Try me."

Lynn visibly stiffened and retreated. "I don't want to fight with you. If you're going to yell at me, I'm leaving."

"Lynn, after all you've put me through, don't you think I deserve an explanation? I don't want to fight. I want to understand."

The girl shrugged. "It's a long story."

"No problem. I've been informed I have a week to hear it."

"Oh, yeah. I missed the plane."

"*You* missed the plane?" Sara asked. "What do you mean? What plane?"

"The one to St. Paul." Again Lynn shrugged. "Rance thought I ought to go back where I came from."

Sara frowned, disconcerted by this new information. "He did?"

"Yeah. I mean, he really wasn't looking for a wife. The whole thing was Tag's idea."

"Tag was looking for a wife? He's only fourteen."

Lynn shook her head, her wet hair spraying Sara with water. "No, no. Tag was looking for a wife for Rance. See, Rance has been really bummed out since Tag's mom died, so Tag thought a new wife might make him happy again. And then maybe he'd let Tag live at home, instead of going to boarding school." She lifted her brows in resignation. "Rance doesn't want to get married again. I heard him tell Tag—kinda stern—that he *never* wanted another wife." She sighed. "Guess he loved his wife a whole lot. But like I said, Rance is a happenin' dude. He wasn't even mad at me or Tag when I showed up here—well, hardly. And he doesn't make us do anything we don't want to do, so I decided I didn't want to go home. So I didn't."

"And he allowed that?" Sara asked, horrified. "I can't believe any grown adult would approve of such a thing." She hugged herself, trying to ward off a shudder. She didn't know if it was her damp clothes, the relief of finding her sister healthy, or the strain of all those days of uncertainty that was making her body quake with reaction.

Or could it be irritation at Rance Shepard for neglecting to let anyone in Andover, Kansas, know that Lynn was alive and well? Even though Lynn had told him she had no family, he should have contacted the Andover police to make sure. How could he have ignored his responsibility? By being so remiss, he'd allowed Sara to worry herself to distraction. She had to admit, though, that knowing he wasn't the dirty old man she pegged him to be made her feel a little less hostile toward him. Not much—nothing you could detect without a microscope—but a little.

"Well, you can't really blame Rance, sis. I told him I was from Detroit." Lynn grinned sheepishly. "Funny, how he couldn't find out anything when he called the Detroit police."

Sara's mouth dropped open in shock. "You...you lied."

Unrepentant, Lynn giggled, "And I, uh, well, never mind, you're cold." Patting her big sister's arm, she suggested, "Let's go inside."

Chagrined by Lynn's lack of remorse, Sara's anger resurfaced. "How could you do that? How could you let me worry? Didn't you know I'd be out of my mind? You acted *so* irresponsibly. I don't know when I'll be able to pay off that credit-card bill." Grasping Lynn's shoulders, she admonished, "And I had to use up all our savings to get here. What possessed you to pull this crazy stunt?"

Lynn's expression grew stony. "Don't yell at me. Rance doesn't yell. He knows I'm grown up. He lets me make my own decisions."

"Considering your recent decisions, I'm not sure he's wise to trust you to make any decisions at all."

Shoving Sara's hands away, Lynn shouted, "I don't care what you think. It took me two days of sleeping in airports and flying standby to get here, but I did—*all by myself*—so get off my back. I'm not a baby anymore."

"Listen to me, young lady, I may not be your mother, but since I've been the one to put food in your mouth and clothes on your back for the past eight years, I think I deserve some respect."

"That's *your* problem."

Sara stared, stunned. "When did you become such a brat?" she whispered. "I can't believe I've raised you this badly."

"Chill out, sis, 'cause I'm *through* being raised," Lynn snapped. "I'm on my own now, so why don't you cruise on back to Kansas and leave me alone." Without another word, she bounded over Sara's overnight case and threw open the door. A second later it was slammed shut, leaving Sara alone on the porch. All further sound was overwhelmed by the pelting of rain against the wood shingles.

Sara's teeth began to chatter. Even this early in June, the thermometer in Kansas had been hovering around ninety when she'd left Andover yesterday. As far as she was concerned, it was freezing here. She could do with a little of that Midwest sunshine about now.

She glanced back over her shoulder at the door. Although it had been slammed, it hadn't quite latched and now stood open an inch—almost taunting her to enter. She should; she had no other choice. But she couldn't. She needed time to calm down so she wouldn't throttle Lynn. She loved her sister, but at the moment she was having a hard time finding anything likable about her.

Besides, she didn't want to confront Ransom Shepard again just yet. She'd been rash and unreasonable with him, and she was ashamed of herself. And she was going to have to spend the next week as his houseguest! The idea made her cheeks go hot with embarrassment.

After several minutes of getting more and more chilled staring at the curtain of rain cascading past the open door to the porch, she sank down onto her overnight case. Wrapping her arms around herself to combat the cold, she acknowledged that she was going to have to go inside and behave like a mature adult eventually. Sitting out here alone probably appeared childish and stubborn to Rance Shepard. But she had to think, calm herself.

She'd been frightened out of her wits for nine days—an eternity filled with doubt and dread. Now that she knew Lynn was not hurt, *not* married and not even, er, sharing some man's bed, she could begin to breathe easily, mend her tattered spirit. With a ragged sigh, she rested her face in her hands. She didn't know what to do about Lynn's selfish mouthy behavior, and she was afraid she owed Mr. Shepard an apology—two mammoth obstacles to her immediate peace of mind and well-being.

The din of the rain suddenly seemed staccato and very loud, no longer just a dull backdrop to her predicament. Perhaps highly stressful situations unblocked the senses allowing heightened perception. Whatever the reason, the storm was now far from an indistinct entity in her mind as it smashed against the earth and battered the shingles without mercy. She shivered, knowing how the earth and the porch must feel; her emotions had been battered around quite a bit lately, too.

And as the disquieting face of Ransom Shepard appeared in her mind's eye, the chill within her deepened.

CHAPTER TWO

SHE DIDN'T LIKE HIS LOOKS. Well, she *did* like his looks, but that was exactly the problem. Something had to be wrong with a man who looked so perfect. No man who *looked* perfect ever really was. Sara might have been only twenty-five, but she'd met a lot of good-looking men in her waitressing jobs, and she'd learned they were usually after one of two things: sex or money. They either wanted a quick meaningless fling, or they were so involved in their careers they didn't have time for a relationship. Which category Mr. Ransom Shepard fell into she had yet to discover. He didn't appear to be driven by a career. Though his house was slightly larger than the others she'd seen on the island, it was certainly no palace. And there was no industry on St. Catherine, except possibly some fishing.

She swallowed. Casual sex, then? No, that didn't appear to be the case—at least not with teenage girls. For that, Sara was extremely grateful. Lynn's words came back to her—"He never wanted another wife." Grief, then, was part of the reason he was here. He was still grieving over the loss of his first wife. She heaved a long sigh. Grief she could understand. Maybe it wouldn't be so bad being here; it was only for a week, after all.

But grief didn't account for everything. There was something else strange—and troubling—about him. She could feel it. Possibly he was simply one of those people who couldn't stand the pressures of the corporate world—some sort of hippie. But he didn't dress like a hippie, and he didn't appear to be a man who'd fold under pressure. She frowned, puzzled. Time would tell the nature of his imperfection, she supposed.

She was perched on her overnight case, her arms wound around her protectively as she watched the rain drench the hilly landscape. Her teeth chattered together with reckless disregard for their survival. In self-defense, she clamped her jaws tight, trying to ignore the cold as it seeped further and further into her bones. But as she slowly froze to death, she also slowly regained her composure.

She canvassed the emerald landscape, managing a weary smile. St. Catherine Island looked like prehistoric Ireland, but without a single tree. Though she'd never been to Ireland—prehistoric or otherwise—this is what she thought it might have looked like: green meadows splashed with colorful flowers, unspoiled by human hands. This place truly had the feel of a rainwashed paradise, albeit a chilly one.

She swiped at her hair. The dampness was starting to make it curl. In a few more minutes she'd look like an overgrown Shirley Temple, her shoulder-length hair corkscrewing around her face in mutinous abandon. "Oh, well," she mused tiredly, "who am I trying to impress, anyway?"

The door to the house squeaked at her back, and she tensed. Stifling a shudder, she brushed a hand through her tangled mane. "I—I'll be just a minute," she mumbled, too embarrassed to turn around to see who was there.

She was jolted by a tug at her hair. Before she could snap her head around, she felt another tug. This time the yank was hard enough to hurt.

"Hey! I know I was a little hotheaded before, but I don't deserve to be manhandled," she protested, swinging her shoulders and head around to face her attacker.

With her mouth opened to object further, she met dark gold eyes, set above a thin, nut-brown muzzle. Whatever confronted her was practically all legs and stood at least four feet tall. Sara didn't know what the creature was, but having been bitten by a dog once long ago, a sudden stark terror swept through her. Before she could move, the thing bared brilliant white teeth, less than two inches from her nose and gave off a menacing high-pitched cry. The threat so startled her that she toppled off the overnight case, landing on her back. Screaming she lifted her hands to ward off an attack, but instead of leaping on her, the lanky monster stumbled backward and disappeared into the house.

Sara stared, wide-eyed, still in a state of shock, and stuttered, "Wh-what was that?"

"That was Boo," a deep voice answered from the door.

Sara shifted to see Ransom towering there, a wry smile tugging at his mouth. "Boo's one of our pets."

She swallowed. "Some pet," she rasped weakly. "It was going to eat me. What was it?"

"An orphaned reindeer. I'm afraid you frightened him quite badly, Miss Eller."

"*I* frightened him?" she echoed in disbelief. "He *snarled* at me, Mr. Shepard. And took a bite out of my hair. I was the attackee, not the attacker."

"Are you all right?" he asked softly.

Sara shoved herself up onto her elbows. "I'll live. How can you keep such a dangerous beast around?"

Ransom allowed himself a small chuckle. "He's only two months old. I would no more turn him out than I would you."

She glowered at him, unable to form an answer.

"The only difference is," he added, his tone taunting. "I like reindeer."

She made a disgusted face. "Why don't you try for *real* subtlety and just kick me."

"That would be ungentlemanly."

"Are you intimating that being ungentlemanly would be a stretch for you?"

He eyed her with mild interest, her insult obviously rolling off his back. "Are you comfortable?" he asked at last.

"Why? Don't I look comfortable?" She was sprawled on the porch floor shivering uncontrollably, disheveled and frightened out of ten years' growth. He'd have to be a dolt to believe she was anything but miserable.

His eyes began to glimmer with an odd light, as though he was amused about something. "Would you care for a hand up?"

"Don't go out of your way, Sir Galahad," she mumbled, struggling to a sitting position.

He rubbed a fist across his lips. Sara wondered if he was hiding a smile. Oh, what difference did it make? She had to live with the man for a week. Let him laugh at her if he must. She'd survive; she'd survived worse. Why not try to make the best of a bad situation? With a groan, she admitted, "To be honest, I think I've had enough of... the great outdoors for one day."

"It's noon."

"Don't remind me. I'm starving." Rubbing her bruised hip, she started to stand and found herself being assisted by a hand at her elbow.

"We have food."

"But you also have a man-eating reindeer."

"Two, actually."

"*Two* reindeer live in your house?" Sara was so flabbergasted she almost laughed, murmuring under her breath, "Toto, I don't think we're in Kansas anymore."

"They don't actually live in, they only visit."

"And play cards on rainy days, I suppose?" she asked.

His indolent grin was charming, though she hated to admit it.

"There, you see?" he remarked. "We're not so different from Kansans. I bet you play cards on rainy days, too."

"Oh, sure. Me, Lynn and a couple of cows."

"Is that any way to talk about your girlfriends?"

She examined his rakish profile. "Very funny. But what about these bullying reindeer? How do I keep from becoming a plate of hors d'oeuvres?"

"Baby's a female, Boo's sister. You don't need to be afraid—both of them are as gentle as kittens. Probably more so, considering that many of the cats on our islands are wild."

"Oh, fine. Your cats are wild, but huge hulking reindeer live in houses? Interesting place."

"Actually, neither are native to the islands. The cats were brought over in the twenties from Alaska as pets while the reindeer were imported from Siberia ten years later as livestock."

"Livestock with an attitude," she muttered. "Besides I never said I was afraid."

"Oh? Then I presume that scream I heard was primal in nature. A cleansing of your psyche perhaps?"

She saw the amused gleam in his eyes and gave up. "Okay. You've made your point. But before we get within earshot of the kids, I want to make a point of my own."

He inclined his head. "I'm listening."

"First—" she cleared her throat nervously "—I'm sorry about the way I behaved earlier. I misunderstood some things...."

He nodded. "It's forgotten. And second?"

She chewed her lower lip for a time before she could go on. "Don't mistake me, Mr. Shepard. I know Lynn lied and told you she was from Detroit. But I think if you'd really tried, you could have found out her identity. Through my credit card, for instance. You were derelict in your duty as a parent by not trying harder to notify authorities in Andover, Kansas, that she was alive and well. I'm going to have a hard time forgiving you for that."

The amusement in his eyes died. A fleeting look of sorrow replaced it, confusing Sara. Quickly that emotion, too, was gone, and his expression mirrored his matter-of-fact tone. "This may come as a shock, Miss Eller, but I'm not looking for your forgiveness."

Sara felt new irritation flood through her at his lack of concern. She couldn't abide people who had no sense of responsibility. Apparently Ransom Shepard was an idle recluse who had plenty of money and nothing to do all day but follow his own self-absorbed whims. She, on the other hand, had been forced to fend for herself and her little sister since their parents had died. She'd worked at any menial job—sometimes two and three at a time—to keep them from starving. And this contemptible scoundrel didn't care about anything—least of all her feelings.

She put ice into her tone as she retorted, "I would tell you I don't think I'm going to like you, Mr. Shepard, but I gather you'd say you don't care."

"Congratulations, Miss Eller. You're learning." He smiled then. It was cold, though his eyes shone with a brooding emotion. Something told Sara he was infuriated by her reprimand, but chose to hide it. "By the way," he suggested, his own voice flinty, "if you can find that credit card, I'll eat it. My guess is Lynn threw it in the sea before she got here."

"You're saying you looked for it?" she demanded.

"Your little sister was very resourceful in making sure her tracks were covered. Happy now?"

She stared blankly, recalling that Lynn had stopped in midsentence before revealing something. Had she been about to admit she'd thrown the credit card in the ocean? Undoubtedly. A new apology wavered unsaid on her lips, but she couldn't bring herself to speak.

"Apology accepted," he chided, as though he'd read her mind.

Still, she could only watch his devilish flash of teeth, finding it difficult to ignore his appeal. Chastened, her face burning with mortification, she preceded him into the house. She knew she had no choice at this point—unless she wanted to remain outside and die of hypothermia.

After a couple of steps, she stumbled to a stop, repelled by what she saw. The stone entry hall was littered with the debris of day-to-day living. Magazines were tossed hither and yon amid a grimy haze of neglect.

The interior clearly had once been attractive. Wood-paneled walls were adorned with dust-covered Aleut and Russian artifacts. A fire blazed warmly on a massive stone hearth at the end of the living room, but the carved-wood-and-leather furniture was strewn with newspapers and dirty laundry. Most appalling of all, a gangling reindeer was curled up on one end of the sofa, making little grunting sounds in her sleep. On the end nearest Sara, two liquid eyes peered over the clothes that had been strewn along the couch's arm; those eyes—Boo's—studied her warily.

Sara squinted with disbelief. "Those...animals are on the couch!" she exclaimed. "You let livestock sleep on the furniture on these islands?"

"No, I think Tag and I are the only ones who do," he answered with a wry grin.

Casting her gaze about, she couldn't believe what she saw. "Why, you live like a pig," she declared under her breath, not realizing until the words were out that she'd spoken.

"I'm sorry, Miss Eller, I didn't quite catch that," he remarked close to her ear.

Wheeling to face him, she felt her cheeks flush. She hadn't meant to say such a rude thing. Thinking fast, she sputtered, "I, er, was wondering if I could have glass of, uh..."

"Pig?" he finished for her, letting her know he'd heard every word.

She flushed again. "I didn't mean to offend you. But I've never seen anything like this place." She spread her arms in a helpless gesture. "It looks as though you've been burglarized." Then she asked almost hopefully, "Have you been burglarized?"

"We have no thieves on St. Catherine Island. What you see is what you get. Your sister, however, seems to enjoy the neo-burglarized ambiance of the place."

With an unhappy shake of her head, Sara said, "I'm sure she does. And I'd enjoy being able to order in pizza three times a day. But a person can't live like that."

"Not here, anyway. No pizza parlors. No burger joints. No restaurants."

"No brooms? No mops? No *disinfectant?*"

"I wouldn't know." His grin was disconcerting.

She gaped at him, shaking her head. "I-I know it isn't my business, but this is a repulsive way to live."

"You're absolutely right," he said quietly.

She peered back at him. "I'm glad you agree with me."

"I do." He nodded. "It isn't any of your business."

At a loss, she braced herself and did a slow complete circle to take in the devastation. A sound drew her attention, and she picked her way through the mine field of scattered books, newspapers, dishes and shoes to look into the living room. At the far right, the entrance to the kitchen could be seen. Lynn and Tag were busy doing something but it was definitely not cleaning up.

She plunged toward them her eyes darting restlessly about as if the place were alive with demons. There was a bookshelf on the wall opposite the fireplace. A pair of jeans dangled from the top shelf, as did several mismatched socks. A dirty plate and glass tottered atop a dictionary. Grimacing, Sara cautiously entered the kitchen, where the countertops were piled high with dishes and the debris of discarded meals.

"What in heaven's name is going on here?" she asked, not wanting to believe her own eyes. "What are you two doing?"

Lynn looked at Sara with some caution. "We're eating lunch."

Sara stared, dumbfounded. Between them they held two opened tin cans. They were digging into them, eating directly from one another's tin. Sara blanched. "What is it?" she asked, her voice high-pitched in anxiety.

"Salmon and peaches," Tag offered. Then with a small grin, he said, "I don't think we've met. I'm Tag Shepard."

Nodding uncertainly, Sara managed a weak, "Hello, Tag." Moving her gaze to Lynn, she couldn't help but plead, "What has gotten into you? This . . . this is a bizarre nightmare! Do you realize it'll take me years to repay the bills you charged getting here? And to do what? Eat out of cans and live like a savage? What about nursing school? You can't possibly go now, not unless you work a couple of years after high school first. What possessed you to do such a crazy thing?"

Lynn stopped chewing and banged her can down on the messy table. "You wanna know why I ran away?" she shouted, her expression mutinous. "Why I wanted to marry a rich man and live far, far away from you and Kansas?"

Sara nodded, but she wasn't sure she wanted to hear this, not now, not with an audience. Still, she couldn't voice an objection. She'd been waiting nine terrible days and nights to understand why Lynn had run away. She loved her younger sister more than anything in the world, and she'd worked hard so Lynn's life could be better than her own. "Yes, I want to understand..." She allowed the sentence to drift away.

"I'll tell you, then." Lynn's stare was hard. "Because I don't want to end up like you. A *nothing!* Don't kid yourself. We can barely make ends meet—do you really think that, even with us both working I can ever scrape enough together to pay for nursing school? I ran away 'cause I don't want to end up poor and worn-out! You're twenty-five, and you look years older. You're exhausted all the time. You don't have a life—"

"Lynn!"

All eyes swung toward Ransom, who'd spoken that one sharp word and then said nothing more.

"What?" Lynn asked, her petulant tone fading only slightly.

A grin lifted his lips, but didn't touch his eyes. Sara had the feeling it was a token effort. She also had the feeling he'd been about to reprimand her sister, but then thought better of it. When he spoke, his voice held none of its former rancor. "The rain's stopped. Why don't you kids wake Baby and take her and Boo outside?"

Sara watched him for another second. He seemed so calm and uncaring now. Maybe she'd imagined everything.

"Okay, Rance." Lynn eyed her sister angrily for a moment, then turned to Tag. "Where'll we go?"

"Let's get my Cubs cap and go down to the beach. Maybe that dolphin, Potluck, will be there. He loves to steal my cap and take it around to Sea Lion Cove. That'll give Boo and Baby a good run."

Lynn smiled. "Okay. Great."

Looking at his dad, Tag asked, "Where's my cap?"

Ransom's shrug was elegantly casual. "Wouldn't know, pal."

"I think I saw it sticking out of the cookie jar," Lynn said.

They recovered it and were halfway out of the kitchen when Ransom asked, "By the way, kids, what would you like for dinner?"

They brightened noticeably.

"Fried chicken," Tag shouted.

"Spaghetti," Lynn cried, poking Tag in the ribs. "You like spaghetti," she whispered loudly to the boy.

"Okay, spaghetti," Tag agreed with a definite nod.

"Sounds good to me." Indicating the kitchen with a broad gesture, Ransom added, "You'll find all the ingredients in the cupboard."

The light went out of their expectant eyes. "Ah, you always make us fix our own dinner," Tag groused, settling the baseball cap low on his brow.

"That way you eat exactly what you want," Ransom said easily. "See you two later."

"Later," they mumbled as they exited the kitchen.

Sara barely noticed their departure. She was hurting too badly. Casting her gaze to the floor, she hoped Ransom couldn't see the pain caused by Lynn's cruel insult glistening in her eyes.

"She didn't mean what she said," he offered in an unexpectedly gentle tone. "Kids can be pretty self-centered."

Sara hated the pity in his voice. "You ought to know," she charged hoarsely, glaring at him. "You're no better than they are—totally lacking any sense of responsibility. How could you allow them to live like this?"

A shadow crossed his face, then was promptly gone. In its place blossomed a contrary grin. "There you go again, trying to make me give a damn about what you think."

She frowned, but didn't have time to object before he went on. "Miss Eller, we have very few rules around here. If you want to eat, feed yourself, and if you want clean clothes, wash them yourself. Understand?"

"I understand," she said, her tone as detached as his had been.

"Fine. Now I've got an errand to run."

As he ambled from the kitchen, her heart sank. What had Lynn gotten them into? This house of his was a living, breathing bad dream, and she didn't think pinching herself was going to get her out of it. Distraught, she sighed. It would take a bulldozer to make this place livable. Pushing up her sleeves, she started to gather dishes.

"What do you think you're doing?" came a deep demand from the living room.

"Washing dishes."

"Don't touch those."

"I refuse to live like a bum."

He reappeared at the door, his eyebrows pulled together in a fierce scowl. "I don't make a habit of explaining myself to people I hardly know. Suffice it to say, I have good reasons for living like this."

"Good reasons!" she exclaimed. "I'd be glad to hear one good reason for living like a lazy pack rat!"

She began to chafe beneath his scrutiny before he finally spoke. "You're only going to be here a week. Don't interfere. Touch a single plate, and you'll sleep on the beach."

"At least it's clean on the beach."

"And it's near freezing at night," he said flatly, clearly trying to control his temper. "I won't warn you again. Leave my house and my things alone."

She glared at him, totally frustrated. "You're nuts, you know!"

"My mental condition is none of your business, and neither is the condition of my house. You and Lynn are unwelcome guests. Keep that in mind," he cautioned, signaling an end to the discussion.

She took a rebellious step forward, refusing to be bullied. "We're also *unwilling* guests!"

"Speak for yourself."

She'd never in her life met a man who was so hard to reason with. But she had to admit he had a point. This was his house. She supposed he could live like a pig if it pleased him. Feeling defeated, she sagged against the cluttered table. A tin can rolled off, clattering along the tile floor. Through clenched jaws, she uttered an unladylike word.

"Such talk," he rebuked from a distance.

Her face grew hot. She'd had no idea that her voice would carry all the way into the living room. "I hope it makes you happy to know you can drive a person to using bad language," she grumbled aloud.

"Ecstatic." The slamming of the door told her that he was gone.

Sara forced herself to walk around the house to view the entire, throat-clutching mess. Without a doubt, she now knew this man's great failing. He was a slob—a stubborn, shiftless, self-absorbed slob. Lynn and Tag had truly found themselves a paradise. Sara, on the other hand, had tumbled headlong into hell.

SARA SPENT the afternoon avoiding Ransom Shepard like the plague. She'd glimpsed him on his return from his errands; he'd been driving a red Jeep filled with boxes. She'd found out from Tag that they were supplies left by the plane she'd flown in on, as well as gas for the generator and mail. The Jeep was Ransom's. There was a garage out back, which she hadn't noticed upon her arrival, that also housed the generator.

It was nearly five o'clock now, and cloudy. A fog was rolling in from the sea, and Sara, out for a walk, hugged herself. Though she'd managed to scrounge a man's down jacket from the hall closet, she still felt the damp chill. Glancing up toward the house, she grimaced. The last thing she wanted to do was go back to that cluttered place and spend time with that irritating man.

"Hi."

She jumped, whirling to see the very same irritating man standing before her.

"Everything okay?" he asked as though they were old friends and had never argued a day in their lives.

Sara stared at him. What could be okay? She stuffed her hands into her coat pockets and shrugged dejectedly. "Are you sure there isn't any other way off this island?" she asked, turning to gaze at the sea.

"I've been working on it all afternoon. Unfortunately we've had another burnout at our earth station satellite."

She looked back at him doubtfully. "Does that mean the Martians are on the warpath?"

He almost smiled. "Cute. But no. It means no phones until we can order the part. And we can't order a part until old Krukoff gets here next Wednesday."

"Great," she muttered.

"Too bad the rescue boat's out of the question."

That remark straightened her spine with anticipation. "What do you mean? Why, for heaven's sake?" she demanded. "It could take us to St. Paul. That's only forty miles away."

He shook his head, looking almost as if he understood her distress. "It's a *rescue* boat. What would we do if someone needed it while it was ferrying you around? What if one of our fishing boats began to sink, and our fishermen were bobbing about in the sea, freezing?"

"Oh. How often does that happen?"

"Not often."

"Well?" She spread her arms in silent appeal. "If it doesn't happen often, why can't we take the chance?"

"Sporting of you to offer, but it's not your life you'd be betting on. Besides, it's an old boat. Probably couldn't make it the forty miles—especially in this fog."

She frowned, then had another thought. "What about one of the fishing boats? It doesn't have to be right now. What if I offered to pay someone to take us to St. Paul in the morning?"

He nodded, giving her hope. "To somebody from Kansas, that must sound dandy. But our boats Miss Eller, are twenty-six-foot, open inboard-outboards, with iffy VHF radios that don't charge properly—not to mention no radar. Even seasoned fishermen wouldn't take them that far, not even on a clear calm day. They're just not fit to travel forty miles out to sea. Besides, you folks from Kansas with all those oil wells may not know this, but for a lot of us, gas is expensive. Still, I have to admit I'd pay the tab for renting a damned boat—if it was possible."

She bristled. "Kansans are aware of the price of gas, thanks. I don't appreciate being patronized."

His lips twitched. "Forgive me," he said, his tone amused and openly insincere.

She eyed him critically. "For a man who takes in orphaned reindeer, you have a real mean streak."

"I know you're not happy," he said more seriously. "Don't you think I would have gotten you off the island if there'd been a way?"

She studied his grave face, then gave a disheartened nod.

"We may as well have a truce." He extended one hand.

She blinked, surprised. With more reluctance than she'd expected to feel, she placed her fingers in his. She was startled to find his hand so warm. Feeling curiously as though she was doing something illicit, she withdrew her fingers, saying rather huskily, "I'm sorry about . . . you know—everything. It isn't my business how you live your life."

He examined her closely. "You mean that, don't you."

"Yes. I am sorry." She sensed a softening in his attitude and decided to try for a compromise. "But couldn't we maybe have one cleanup day? It'd make the place livable, and help the kids develop responsibility toward—"

"This cleanup day worked for you and Lynn, did it?"

Sara glanced away in embarrassment. "Not too well. I tried to get her to help, but you know how kids are."

"As a matter of fact, I do," he assured her, his tone suddenly edged with steel. "And I'd appreciate it if you'd allow me to handle my own life in my own way."

"But you're not—"

"Living up to your idea of a good parent?"

She considered his stony expression. "What's the use? You already know what I think."

"So, we're back to square one."

"I suppose."

When he said nothing more, she began to move away down the beach.

After only a few steps, she heard him ask, "What if I told you I was using reverse psychology on the kids—making their lives so miserable they'll be forced to take some responsibility."

She stopped and half turned. "Well, since they're far from miserable, I'd say you were goading me again. I'd also say that if there was an Olympic event for sarcasm, you'd be a gold medalist."

He lifted a rueful eyebrow. "I can't put anything over on you, can I?"

Irritated by his teasing, she resumed her walk into the fog.

"What's with your hair, Miss Eller?" he called. "It wasn't curly when you first got here. Does it just do that when it's wet?"

She swung back. "Why? Isn't it messy enough for your taste?"

He chuckled. "Actually, yes. It's messy enough."

She heaved a sigh, irked that she'd stumbled right into that one. "You're in a fine mood."

"Not really, but I do like your hair that way."

He turned and strolled off, leaving Sara standing alone, annoyed and puzzled. She took hold of the end of a curl and pulled it straight down in front of her eyes. Letting go, the strand corkscrewed back against her forehead. *He likes it this way?* He was being sarcastic, she decided. He was never serious about anything. Didn't care about anything. What a bum!

She glared at Ransom's back as he walked leisurely off, his hands in the pockets of his leather bomber jacket. He was a wholly eccentric man, a crazy man no woman in her right mind would have anything to do with.

As she watched him disappear into the fog, she mumbled under her breath, "You're nuts, Ransom Shepard." Inwardly her little voice said, *He may be nuts, but, unfortunately that doesn't stop him from being heart-stoppingly attractive.*

CHAPTER THREE

IT WAS AFTER TEN, and the world outside was still bright with unrelenting daylight. Hours ago, Sara had cleared a spot on the couch and spent the evening thumbing through magazines. A sound caught her attention. She glanced up to see Ransom carrying a couple of kerosene lanterns, and she squinted in confusion.

"Expecting a power outage?" she asked, having decided to honor the truce and be as pleasant a guest as possible, considering the miserable circumstances.

He looked at her, his expression somehow amused. "Actually, yes. Every night at ten I turn off the generator to conserve fuel." His eyes roamed over her as she sat in her cozy little nest, but he gave away nothing of his thoughts. "Usually we go to bed at ten. Even though the sun doesn't set until twelve-thirty, it rises at four."

She lay her magazine in her lap, facing him. "I work a split shift in Kansas—the lunch crowd at a diner, then the dinner crowd in a club. I don't get off till two in the morning. I may have a little trouble adjusting to bed at ten."

"I don't think so," he said. "We're on Bering Standard Time. In Kansas it's after one o'clock in the morning now."

Her brows dipped, but she couldn't stifle a yawn. "I thought it was stress that was making me so tired."

His friendly grin was unexpected. "No, it's fairly late, even for you." Handing her one of the lamps, he said, "Keep this. If you need to get up during the night. Light it.

It's not dark for long, but with the curtains drawn, it's *very* dark."

Taking it, she uncurled herself and stood, surveying the room. The driftwood fire was dying on the hearth, and Lynn and Tag were nowhere to be seen. "Where are the kids?" she said, almost to herself.

"Probably over at Doc Stepetin's place. He has a TV."

"Doesn't Dr. Stepetin turn off his generator?"

"The rest of the island homes are on one generator. They keep it going all the time."

"When do the kids have to be back?"

"Whenever they care to."

She felt the urge to debate the wisdom of that, but said nothing. He'd made his opinion clear on the subject of her butting in. Still, Lynn was *her* sister. She decided to remind him of that fact. "I realize you have rules here—which basically means no rules at all—but, I'd like you to let me establish some guidelines for my own flesh and blood, even if we are under your roof."

"She rebelled against your guidelines, if you recall. What do you want her to do—run away to the North Pole?"

Sara hadn't expected him to be so blunt, and she felt her eyes sting with moisture. Apparently she was more tired than she'd realized. She didn't usually burst into tears because someone found fault with her. Waitresses had to take all kinds of verbal abuse from all kinds of rude and thoughtless people. Her anxiety over this whole mess must be getting to her.

Maybe learning to take abuse from thoughtless customers with a smile was partly to blame for Sara's current problems. Could it be that because she'd tried to ignore rude remarks, she'd allowed her sister to talk back too often, get away with too much? Maybe Sara should have been more strict with her. She'd obviously made a mess of trying to be a mother to Lynn. With that unhappy thought, Sara mumbled, "I don't care to fight, Mr. Shepard. Call it fatigue, call it cowardice if it makes you feel superior. Right now, I simply want to go to bed."

He frowned, and Sara had the feeling his irritation was directed more at himself than at her. Without further comment, he motioned toward the doorway that was midway between the fireplace and the kitchen. It led to a hall. On the left was the master bedroom, where Ransom slept. Next was the bathroom. Then there were two more bedrooms. He indicated the room at the other end of the hallway. "This is Lynn's room. Since we're starting to pile up here, I'm afraid you two will have to share."

"No problem," she murmured, grateful at least that she'd be a hallway's length from him.

"I'll be right back," he said. "Better get some matches for the lantern. They're in that stone urn on the mantel."

As she reached the mantel above the fireplace the electric light by the couch went out.

Clutching the book of matches she'd retrieved, she was reentering the hallway when Ransom returned.

"Do you have anything to sleep in?" he asked, surprising her.

Not having much room in her overnight case, she'd only packed a light cotton nightie. Her plans hadn't included a week's stay on a remote subarctic island. She shook her head and, not wanting to discuss her nightclothes with this man, said, "I'll make do."

"Even with our coal furnace, it gets cool at night. I'll find you something." He went into his room. After a minute, he was back with a man's flannel shirt. It was hanging on a wooden hanger and looked fresh from the laundry.

She inspected it, deciding the dim hallway light couldn't be playing that big a trick on her. Not only was the shirt clean and pressed, but it was protected by a plastic bag. She'd never seen flannel look quite so pristine. Taking it from him, she teased, "I can see why you'd want to get rid of this stain on a life-style of grime and clutter."

His gaze grew inhospitable. "You're welcome, Miss Eller." With a curt nod, he turned away. "Sleep well."

"Uh, I'm sorry," she called, feeling thoroughly put in her place. "I didn't mean—"

He was gone, secluded behind his closed door, before she could finish. Ashamed, she bit her lip, wondering what she might have said if he'd stopped and acted as though he cared.

She stood there, staring at the shirt. Her stomach growled. She hadn't eaten anything for dinner, not quite knowing what to do, considering the squalor of the place. Lynn and Tag had opened a can of salmon and one of baked beans, opting for another easy, if not nutritionally balanced, meal. Sara had felt a little sick to her stomach watching them, and she'd retreated to the living room to forcibly duck her nose into a news magazine.

She'd heard pleasant chatter and laughter from the kitchen and was aware that Ransom had fixed himself a sandwich. She'd watched covertly as he'd gathered up his dishes. For a moment, she'd heard water running, and had a surge of hope that he was washing them. But quickly the sound stopped. Dejected, she'd settled back to try to read. She must have dozed off, because the next thing she knew, it was minutes ago and Ransom was towering above her holding the lanterns.

A shuffling on the porch drew her attention. The front door clicked open, and Sara heard the familiar sound of Tag and Lynn's laughing banter as they came in.

Sara went to the entrance to the living room. When Lynn saw her, she asked, "Still up?"

Keeping her tone as pleasant as possible, Sara said, "I'm going to bed. And you?"

Lynn nodded. "Yeah." Turning to Tag, she said, "See you in the morning."

He retrieved the other lantern and nodded. "Night."

Once cloistered in their bedroom, Sara perched on the edge of one of the twin beds. It was littered with dirty clothes, several odd shoes and a pile of magazines, but the bed was made. The other twin was a wreck. Clearly that was the one her sister had occupied during the past week.

Lynn plopped down next to Sara and whispered conspiratorially, "Couldn't tell you this with Tag around, but I think Rance is a little crazy."

A shaft of unease knifed through Sara as she darted her sister a worried look. Granted, she, too, had accused him of being "nuts," but she hadn't been really serious. "Crazy?" She placed the lantern and matches on the bedside table, then lowered her voice. "What do you mean, crazy?"

"Well," Lynn whispered, acting as though she were about to reveal a huge indiscretion. "You should see his closet!"

Sara cringed, visualizing whips and chains. "Oh, my..." She tugged nervously at her collar. "What does he have in there?"

"It's spotless," Lynn confided. "I mean everything is neat and in order. Like...like it was a magazine article about clean closets or something."

Sara sat back, staring at her sister. "His closet is neat?"

Lynn nodded, her eyes wide and expectant.

"Neat?" Sara repeated, disbelief creeping into her tone. "You think he's crazy because his closet is neat?"

Lynn pouted, flopping back on the bed and propping herself on her elbows. "Well, he's not very neat outside the closet. There's something funny about a man who's messy outside a closet, but neat inside a closet."

Sara peered at the flannel shirt that was lying on the pillow—the neat, plastic-covered flannel shirt. "I can see why *you* might think neatness is crazy," she admonished with a wry grin, "but not everyone is alarmed by it."

"But only neat in a closet?" Lynn insisted.

"It is unusual," Sara admitted, wondering about this mild aberrance in Ransom Shepard's behavior. "But I don't think it's anything to panic about. I've never heard of mad-dog killers having overly neat closets." She eyed her sister levelly. "To be perfectly honest, Lynn, neatness isn't generally considered a hideous crime."

Lynn gave her a disgusted smirk. "Okay, be that way. I just figured you ought to know."

"Thanks for the warning." Hooking a finger in the crook of the hanger, she lifted the shirt. "He loaned me this to sleep in. Do you suppose the crazed, neat-closet freak, put poison in his steam iron and the venom will seep into my pores, causing me to die a horrible death before morning?"

Lynn rolled her eyes. "You're *real* funny."

"Actually, I'm *real* tired." With a brief wave to indicate the debris on the bed, she asked, "Do you think you could find someplace else for this stuff so I can get into bed?"

Lynn gave a theatrical groan and shoved the jumble of clothes, shoes and magazines onto the floor. "Happy?" she asked with a sneer.

Sara held her tongue counting to ten. This wasn't the time to start another fight. Instead, she replied, "Let's say, I'm happy you're okay."

Lynn seemed startled, as though she'd expected a reprimand. Visibly relaxing, she threw herself down on her rumpled bedcovers and came very close to smiling. "Ya know?" she said. "It doesn't totally gross me out to see you, either. Good night."

With a helpless chuckle, Sara said, "You should write greeting cards, kid. That's the kind of sticky sentiment a sister loves to hear." Perching on the edge of her bed, she began to strip down to her underwear.

Lynn was undressed and beneath the covers by the time Sara had donned Ransom's flannel shirt. It was huge on her, the hem trailing just above her knees. The fabric was soft and warm against her skin. It smelled nice, too—clean, but with a faint tang of cologne, as though Ransom's masculine scent had permeated everything within his domain. She sniffed a sleeve as she rolled it up to uncover her hands, feeling a sinful delight in being surrounded by his aura. Irritated, she shook her head. What a ridiculous flight of fancy. She must be more exhausted than she'd realized. This man was not someone she could respect enough to *ever* care about, especially not romantically.

As she was about to crawl beneath the covers, Lynn asked, "Whatcha gonna do tomorrow?"

Noticing the light streaming in the the window between their beds, Sara perched on her knees and pulled the heavy curtains closed. The room became black. "First, I'm going to do some laundry."

"Radical! I'm almost out of clothes."

Examining the darkness where her sister lay, Sara got into bed. She experienced a surge of irritation at her sister's blasé attitude about this awkward predicament her selfishness had cast them into, and she retorted flatly, "I'll give you radical. Do your own laundry, Miss Grown-up."

It distressed Sara that she was playing right into Mr. Ransom Shepard's slovenly plan. Or were his plans really that slovenly? She sniffed at his flannel shirt again, almost smiling. It held the scent of warm spices and reminded her of the pipe her father used to smoke, so many years ago. Could Ransom have been even half-serious about his reverse-psychology remark? Could he really be trying to make the kids' lives so miserable they'd have to take responsibility for themselves? She frowned. Surely not. It was an absurd idea, but—

"Bummer," Lynn lamented, breaking into her thoughts. "Nobody does anything for anybody around here."

"Welcome to the real world, sweetie." After the words were out of her mouth, she found her lips twisting in a rueful smile. She was even beginning to sound like Ransom Shepard. What pithy irony! Why, she and Ransom Shepard were as different as... as love and hate. Weren't they?

She stared into the darkness, wondering if there might be just a touch of method in the man's madness.

RANSOM HADN'T BEEN kidding. Dawn broke early in June on the Bering Sea. A shaft of sunlight had found the one small gap between the curtains and was shining directly in Sara's face. She squinted into the painful bright light. Scrutinizing her watch through slitted eyes, she was dismayed to discover that it was barely four-thirty, yet the sun was already climbing boldly into the heavens.

Calculating that it would be seven-thirty in Kansas—not so horribly early—she yawned and sat up in bed. Lynn was still asleep. With a deep sigh, Sara fished her toothbrush, toothpaste and soap out of her overnight case and shuffled, bleary-eyed and barefoot, toward the bathroom.

When she reached her destination, the door was closed. She hesitated. That probably meant someone was inside. As she raised her fist to knock, the door swung wide and she was face-to-face—rather, face to chest—with Ransom. He was wearing a navy, thigh-length terry robe. Below the robe, he wore nothing to disguise his well-muscled legs. He, too, was barefoot. Her breath caught as she scanned the lower portion of his anatomy. It surprised her to note that his solid calves had a captivating allure. She'd never noticed a man's calves before, but his were remarkably engaging.

"Good morning," he said, his voice deep with derisive humor. "I didn't expect to see you up this early."

Her gaze snapped to his face. His hair was damp and lay in dark ringlets across his forehead. His eyes glittered like silver, and his lips were parted, displaying a cynical flash of teeth.

She yawned. "Oh, great. You're a morning person. That's all I need."

"And you're a sourpuss before you have coffee."

She shrugged, unable to deny it.

"I see the shirt fits," he remarked, his tone softly mocking.

"If that's supposed to mean I'm a witch in the morning, I resent it. Of course, I resent the offensive twitter of birds, too, before I have my coffee."

His smile broadened into something almost genuine. "And I try not to find fault before breakfast. Actually, I was kidding about the size of the shirt. It's a little large."

Knowing she looked like some ragamuffin in cast-off clothes, she swept a drowsy gaze down at herself. One of the shirtsleeves had unrolled and hung about six inches past the hand that held her toothbrush and toothpaste. "Don't be silly," she mumbled. "My fairy godmother couldn't have done better."

"Oh?" he said. "Do you have a fairy godmother?"

She yawned again, in part to mask her growing ire. Fully aware he was baiting her, she decided she could be every bit as sarcastic as he. "Of course I have a fairy godmother. I'm here at the ball, aren't I."

His glinting eyes narrowed. "And where, may I ask, is Prince Charming?"

"Buried somewhere under the litter, I'd guess."

"I'm wounded, milady, that you overlooked me as a possibility."

His eyes were twinkling now. Was he intent on embarrassing her? "As a possibility for what?" she said evasively, trying to hide her disquiet. This towering man exuded such arrogant magnetism she found it difficult to keep from constantly blushing in his presence.

"As a possibility for Prince Charming naturally. Or am I not your type?" he coaxed, his voice soft.

Uncomfortable with their strangely charged repartee, she said rather shortly, "For one thing, I prefer a man with clothes on."

His chuckle had a dry caustic sound. "Isn't that rather Victorian for a woman of the nineties?"

Avoiding his probing gaze, she decided the best course was to drop the subject, so she snapped, "Are you done in there?"

"Forgive me for dawdling." He stepped aside, motioning as gallantly as any prince clad in his bathrobe could. "All yours, Miss Eller. Would you care for some coffee?"

She blinked. "Why, I'd love a cup." Then she frowned. There'd been something about his tone that didn't sit right. Had it been mockery? Of course! When *hadn't* the man mocked her! She lifted her chin. "You're not going to bring me any, are you?"

"Unfortunately the rules forbid it. What would the children say if they found out I was playing favorites?"

His grin was lopsided and dashing, and she had a fleeting thought. Could he be playing some sort of psychological game with her? Was the man made up completely of guile and trickery? Could she believe a word he said, a thing he did? She had no idea if his ploy was to get her to hate him or fall into his arms. Well, she certainly had no plans of doing the latter.

"If it makes you feel any better," he added, breaking through her outraged musings, "I think you're a charming grouch."

She felt a thrill at his unexpected compliment. Then realized that, with the baggy shirt and her hair looking like a nest for bats, she was far from charming. Flustered and irritated with herself for her silly school-girl reaction to his kidding, she muttered, "I probably make better coffee than you ever could, anyway."

One brow rose to meet the damp curls on his forehead. "You think so?"

"I know so. Mine wouldn't have an old sock floating in it."

He laughed shortly. "Touché, Miss Eller. The coffee tin is on the shelf over the percolater. I look forward to a sample."

"I'm not making coffee for you," she retorted. "I can follow rules, too, you know."

He pursed his lips, his eyes holding her in a silvery grip that was suddenly far from amused. "Can you follow *all* rules, or merely the ones that suit you?"

"I—I— What are you talking about?"

He chuckled, a bitter sound. "Nothing. Never mind."

His hooded, unwavering stare so unnerved her that she stumbled backward into the bathroom in a desperate effort to break eye contact. Catching her heel on the mat, she nearly fell. Feeling like an utter fool, she had to summon all her self-control not to slam the door on this strange, hypnotic man.

After she was safely behind the closed door, she had an irrepressible urge to ask him something, something that was gnawing at her, something she sensed every time Ransom's gaze clashed with hers. Poking her head back out, she caught him a second before he entered his room. Out of patience, she challenged, "Is it me, Mr. Shepard, or is it *all* women you hate?"

He twisted around, his eyes flashing, and he appeared about to say something, but then seemed to think better of it. With a determined rotation of his shoulders and two brisk strides, he was inside his room. His door clicked closed once again shutting her out. She pressed her lips together in consternation. Ransom Shepard was beginning to make an irksome habit of stalking away from her.

RANSOM LEFT EARLY that morning to go bird-watching. He's said something about observing the nest-building operations of the red-legged kittiwakes, but she had no idea what tasks that might entail, or how many minutes or, better yet, hours would be involved. So, shortly after he'd gone, Sara searched among the wreckage in the house, discovering clothes that had been hers before Lynn had run away. Apparently her sister had taken with her not only her own things, but a number of Sara's. She set to work washing them, as well as the clothes she'd traveled in. Wandering around in nothing more than Ransom's shirt was embarrassing, but with him away from the house, she didn't feel quite as shameless. She had the distinct feeling her lack of attire had been part of the reason he'd gone off that early. Funny. He'd seemed to recognize her unease and her need for privacy, and had decided to leave her alone. No, surely not. She was reading more into the man's motives then he deserved. He was a bird-watcher, and he'd simply gone bird-watching. That was that.

After she'd done her wash, Sara began to feel that she now had enough clothes to keep from having to traipse about in Ransom's shirt. Tucking the tail of a jasmine-hued blouse into her jeans, both still warm from the dryer, she wandered into the kitchen. Lynn and Tag were opening another can of salmon.

Sara shook her head and said to Lynn, "I had no idea you liked salmon so much."

Her sister giggled without turning away from her work. "Oh, it's okay."

"Okay?" Tag interjected reproachfully, but with a grin. "You dare say my dad's salmon is just *okay?*"

Lynn laughed heartily, tossing the can's lid onto the floor. "Oh, yeah, I forgot. I *love* Bering Sea Salmon more than ice cream and chocolate syrup!" Holding up a can as though she were in a television commercial, she mimicked nasally, "It's tastier than tuna and only costs about half as much as a house!"

They both snickered.

"That's not Dad's slogan, you dork," Tag said. "It's 'Bering Sea Salmon, the Sovereign of the Sea.'"

"I know," Lynn admitted. "When I was little, I thought the TV commercial said, 'Slobbering in the sea.' Yuck!"

They both burst into shrieks of glee, while Sara stood silently watching, confused. "What are you talking about?" she asked when the laughter had subsided.

Tag turned toward her. "Dad's salmon company," he explained. Puffing up his thin chest, he added, "We own the Bering Sea Salmon canneries."

Sara blinked, startled, then once again inspected the wreckage in which this salmon mogul and his son lived. "That can't be," she whispered.

"Uh, huh," Lynn insisted, taking a sliver of the salmon from the can and depositing it into her mouth. "They have four canneries all the way from Juneau to Bethel. Anchorage is where the big dude's offices are."

Sara faced Tag. "Really?"

He nodded, sucking in a piece of salmon.

"Well, why do you live here, then?"

"Oh, this is Ransom's summer place," Lynn explained.

"Yeah. Dad's mom was Aleut." Tag grinned. "I'm one-fourth Aleut, myself. This was the family home. Dad's mom, my grandma Leatha married Keller Shepard, who was in the salmon business. After Grandma passed away, Dad, Mom and I used to come here during summer vacation, and Dad took over counting the birds like Grandma used to do. We stayed here every June—before Mom died. Haven't been here for five years, though." He looked away, appearing self-conscious. "Dad's been pretty busy with the company. But this summer he got me out of the private school where I've been living, and we came here." He smiled sheepishly. "I was being kind of a butt at school."

Lynn nudged him with a hip. "So what's new?"

"Hey!" he retorted. "You should talk. You ain't no Prom Queen yourself!"

They giggled and took turns popping more salmon into their mouths while Sara absorbed what she'd heard. "When did your mother die, Tag?" she asked, unsure if that was a good question, but too curious to let it pass.

Tag sobered. "When I was nine. Car accident."

Sara swallowed, looking at the two of them. Lynn had sobered, too. Her parents had also died in a car accident. It was obvious that Tag and Lynn had become great friends partly because of their similar loses. "So, where do you go to school?" she asked, trying to lighten the mood.

Tag screwed up his face in disgust. "Kirkwood Boys' Prison in Seattle."

"Prison?" Sara repeated. "You look rather young to be in prison."

"Well, *they* call it an academy. I call it a prison."

Sara nodded in understanding. "If it'll make you feel any better, not many young people your age are crazy about school."

"Yeah, but I have to be away all year. Dad didn't even want me to come home at Christmas or—"

"I don't think our guests care to know the family history, Taggart," an authoritative voice interrupted from behind Sara. She spun around to see Ransom in the doorway, his stance almost combative. His features were stern, but enthrallingly so. He wore a cable-knit crewneck sweater. Its color, the soft blue of a Kansas summer sky, set off the silver of his eyes, softening them despite his irritation. A pair of binoculars dangled at his broad chest, and he carried a notebook. Removing the binoculars and swinging them from their strap, he suggested more gently, "It's sunny out. Over fifty degrees. You two should take advantage of the break in the weather."

"Let's take stuff outside and have a picnic," Lynn suggested eagerly.

"I'll get the can opener. You grab food."

After a minute they were gone, leaving Ransom and Sara facing each other. When the quiet had grown uncomfortable, she ventured, "Tag tells me you own Bering Sea Salmon."

Tag and Lynn had left the front door open, and a cold breeze filtered through to the kitchen, bringing with it the tang of the sea. At Ransom's continued silence, Sara breathed deeply of the salty air, hoping to calm her raw nerves. The room was cooling quickly, and she wasn't sure it was completely due to nature's intrusion. There was a chill in Ransom's mood, too.

Why she became so nervous in his presence she couldn't fathom. Averting her gaze, she mumbled, "Never mind. It's none of my business."

She'd started to leave the kitchen when the sound of his voice halted her. "It's no secret," he said.

Curious, she turned back to study him. He was neatly clad, yet he lived in chaos. This lack of self-discipline seemed out of character for a man who owned a multimillion-dollar company. And the order of his closet pestered her thoughts. Maybe there had been more than a little truth to his reverse-psychology comment. Maybe he was really a very sharp intuitive man. Or maybe he was just plain crazy.

All of her misgivings must have shown in her face, for Ransom grinned crookedly. "It's not that interesting a story, Miss Eller," he said, moving past her. His scent mingled with that of the sea, and even in her frustration at never getting a straight answer from him, she found herself inhaling deeply, savoring his unique essence.

Without concrete thought, she perused the messy kitchen. When her gaze fell on an empty can of Bering Sea Salmon, she idly picked it up, turning it in her fingers. She scanned the gold-and-crimson label, so familiar to her. Bering Sea Salmon was the best on the market. She'd even eaten it in Kansas. Not often, but it was there. It was everywhere. Good heavens, Ransom Shepard must have a zillion dollars.

As she set the can down, his last remark came back to mind forcefully—"It's not that interesting a story, Miss Eller." He was wrong. His was a mystery she wanted badly to solve, and it disturbed her to realize she found him so intriguing. She was even attracted to his infuriating laid-back attitude. Whether it was part of his act or part of the real Ransom Shepard she had no idea, but for her to be actually envious of his easygoing manner...!

Sara had never been easygoing, had never had the opportunity. It seemed almost sinful to be so unconcerned about everything. And she was amazed to find that she was enchanted by it—or could it be the *man* who drew her? But was he really easygoing? Would that kind of man send his son off to boarding school? She frowned, skeptical. Or was it possible he was so driven he would go to any radical, deceitful extremes to get his way? She bit down hard on her lip. Heaven forbid! Either way, she didn't need that kind of trouble.

When she looked around for Ransom, she noticed he'd closed the door to the elements and was heading toward his bedroom. Upset, but with no idea what she could do about it, she walked into the living room. Out of the corner of her eye she spied another of her blouses, crumpled heedlessly on the top shelf of an antique oak cabinet. She exhaled dejectedly, wondering how so many clothes had gotten strewn about so wildly.

The cabinet doors were wide open. Deep glass shelves held dusty whatnots and assorted bric-a-brac. When she lifted the blouse away from the shelf, Sara could see that it had been covering the photograph of a woman. Absently she picked up the silver frame and walked with it to the window that faced the open sea.

The woman appeared to be in her mid-twenties, about Sara's age, but her pixie hairstyle was out of current fashion. Her hair was dark brown, her eyes blue. Sara thought she was lovely in a full-figured way. She had generous lips and a soft-featured oval face. Though she wasn't strikingly beautiful, the woman had an interesting face, and Sara knew at once that she was Ransom's late wife.

Out of character for her, Sara felt a rush of dislike for her and had no idea why. Surely it wasn't jealousy. Surely it didn't matter to Sara that this woman had managed to break through the invisible but very real barrier that kept Ransom Shepard from connecting with people—even, it appeared, his own son.

Or perhaps it was the loss of this woman that had done it to him.

"What are you doing?"

Sara was so startled by the harsh male voice behind her she dropped the framed photograph. The glass shattered and, mortified, she sank to the floor to gather up the shards.

"Get away from there," he ordered, pulling her upright. Annoyance sparked in his gaze. "I'll do that."

"I—I'm sorry. I'll replace the..." Her voice faltered and she blushed.

"Forget it," he muttered. Tossing the broken pieces on top of the shattered remnants still in the frame, he eyed her for a heartbeat, his glance made enigmatic by the expansive fringe of his lashes. Before she could say anything else, try to make further amends, he pivoted away.

With rigid strides, he disappeared into the hallway, taking the treasured photo of his wife to the safety of his room. Sara gulped spasmodically, ashamed of her fumble-fingeredness. His pain at the loss of his wife was starkly evident in the coarse emotions she'd witnessed on his face.

Dejected, she retrieved the crumpled blouse from the floor where she'd dropped it, deciding the safest course would be to stay out of Ransom Shepard's way for the next six days—days Sara feared would be the six most difficult of her life.

CHAPTER FOUR

TAG HAD TOLD SARA only that morning that the Pribilof Islands had been dubbed "the birthplace of the winds." At the moment, fighting the elements in her attempt to walk along the foam-strewn beach, she understood why. And she'd thought Kansas had a corner on wind! Here on St. Catherine Island, the gusts were so strong, nothing taller than stunted shrubs could withstand the gale forces that blustered up to ninety miles an hour across the rolling hills of tundra, mosses and subarctic wildflowers.

As Sara climbed the rocky slope that led to Ransom's summer home, she pulled her parka closer about her throat. The sky was cloudy, and the air damp with sea spray. Fog had been thick in the morning, but now, at noon, the weather had grown windy and cold—at least to a Kansan.

Ransom wore no more than a cable-knit sweater when he'd gone out to monitor the red-legged kittiwakes that were building nests at one of his plotted sites on the cliffs. As she'd watched him leave, she'd been filled with misgiving, recalling the strain of the past three days. She couldn't decide what was bothering her. He seemed at ease around the kids, laughing and joking with them. Yet at odd moments, when she happened to catch him unaware, she'd find him staring, features severe and somehow sad, at Tag. That nagged at her. What was wrong between father and son?

But she could do no more than wonder about it, for she was far from being a confidante of Ransom's. It was painfully obvious he not only didn't want her as his friend, he disliked her intensely. Whenever she came into the room, he grew watchful and his stance became rigid. She may have chanced on the discovery that he had a problem with his son—one he was hiding—but he made no bones about his dark feelings for her. They were so palpable a chunk of moss would've had trouble missing them.

Ransom confused Sara. He seemed completely willing to allow the house to fall to ruin around their heads. She decided he might have been kidding when he'd told her he was trying reverse psychology on the kids. He'd probably said that to keep her off his back. In her own defense, she had. But even though she'd quit quibbling about the carnage in the house, he still acted as though she was causing him all sorts of trouble.

Stuffing her hands into her pockets, she wondered for the thousandth time what she could have done to make him dislike her. She'd promised to replace the glass she'd broken in his wife's picture, and she'd silently obeyed his crazy don't-do-anything-for-anybody-else rules. What more did he want? She supposed he simply wanted her and her sister to leave. In the same position, she imagined she'd be every bit as anxious for him to be gone. She sighed despondently. Well, they were in agreement in one area, anyway. Neither of them wanted to spend one more minute with the other than was absolutely necessary.

Movement caught her eye and, stilling, she turned. Over the rise beyond Ransom's house, a man's head appeared. A moment later, as more of him became visible, she could tell he was wearing a suit and was plodding into the wind toward the house. His briefcase wagged in the breeze as he tried to catch his blowing tie. She squinted. Something was wrong with this picture. She didn't think anyone on St. Catherine Island wore a suit and tie.

The man spotted her and altered his course. She hesitated, though she didn't really believe he was a sex maniac or anything. Deciding to assume he was a normal human being, she waited as he approached.

He was rather nice-looking she thought. Probably about thirty-five. His medium brown curly hair was blown back from his forehead, exposing a receding hairline. His round wire-rimmed glasses gave him a successful Yuppie aura. All in all, he appeared to belong on Madison Avenue or Wall Street, not on a far-flung rustic isle in the Bering Sea.

"Hi, there," he said, waving. "I'm looking for Ransom Shepard. Are you a neighbor?"

She shook her head. "No. I'm, um, a... a guest of Ransom's."

His eyebrows darted upward, then he grinned rather strangely. It wasn't a leer, more an expression of pleasure. "Oh? I didn't realize he had guests."

She shrugged, not wanting to go into the details. "It was sort of... last minute."

Releasing his tie and allowing it to flap over his shoulder, he extended a well-manicured hand. "I'm Isaac Dorfman. Ransom's lawyer."

"I'm Sara Eller, from Kansas," she said, slipping her fingers into his. "Ransom's not here right now. He's not back from bird-watching and—"

"Darn. My schedule's pretty tight," he interjected staightening his glasses as he peered at his gold watch. "Could you point me in the right direct—"

"Dorfman!" came a distant shout. "Nothing I'd rather see more right now than your ugly face."

Both Sara and Isaac turned to see Ransom strolling toward them in his unhurried, yet commanding way. Sara swallowed nervously when she saw his wide grin. She'd never seen the smile he reserved for true friends, and she was struck again by his masculine appeal.

Isaac thrust out a hand for Ransom to shake. "You know, no matter how many times I see you with those binoculars and that notebook, it's still hard for me to believe a killer in the boardroom like you counts birds on his vacations. How are Mr. and Mrs. Kittiwake and all the baby Kittiwakes?"

Ransom's grin slackened. "Population's down in two plots. Holding steady in the third. Pretty much in line with my figures of five years ago."

Isaac sighed. "Maybe you should take up a hobby like counting oil spills. They're up."

"You're a sick man, Dorf. Remind me to fire you later," Ransom said with grudging humor. "But right now I'm gladder than hell to see you."

The suited man smiled rather curiously. "I thought you'd bite my head off for bothering you out here, especially on a Saturday."

Flicking Sara a meaningful glance, he shook his head. "You're in luck. I need you. You came in the company plane, didn't you?"

Sara held her breath. *A plane?* She must have been pretty thick not to have realized it. This lawyer was their ticket home!

Dorfman smirked at his boss. "I thought it best to come by plane. It's a damp walk." Holding out his briefcase, he added, "I finally got Wallingford to agree to our terms. But the papers have to be signed and back on his desk by six tonight or the deal falls through."

"We got the whole eleven million?"

Dorfman laughed. "He cried, wheedled, shouted, but in the end, he agreed."

Sara was stunned by the amount of money being bantered around. And she was surprised by Ransom's mild reaction. If *she'd* just made eleven million dollars, she'd be flat on her face in a dead faint. Ransom's smile was lukewarm. What did it take to reach this man?

"That's what I like," Isaac said, looking closely at his boss. "Howling at the top of your lungs and wild applause. I work my little lawyer's brain to a nub and all you can do is give me that nice-to-see-you-what-was-your-name-again smile? I mean, it's eleven million dollars, ol' buddy!"

"That's great," Ransom said absently. "Let's sign the papers. Then I have a couple of passengers for you to take back to Anchorage."

Isaac's expression clouded with confusion. "Passengers?" He shifted the briefcase to under his arm in an attempt to keep it from being buffeted by the wind.

Ransom gestured toward Sara, who hadn't realized she'd unconsciously begun to back away. "I'll...I'll go pack," she murmured. As an afterthought, she said, "And congratulations on your, er, eleven-million thing."

Ransom nodded, but his expression gave no hint of satisfaction over his good fortune. When he said nothing, she hastened to leave, adding, "We'll be ready to go in fifteen minutes."

Hurrying off, she chanced to hear Isaac say to Ransom, "I couldn't be lucky enough for one of your departing passengers to be that gorgeous redhead, could I? Nah. I suppose she's taken."

By his tone, it was clear that Isaac was asking if she and Ransom had a romantic relationship. The idea was so startling she stumbled, but caught herself with a stiffened arm. Standing, she brushed her hands together to knock the grass and dirt from her palm, hoping the men hadn't noticed her misstep.

"Are you hurt?" Ransom called.

She cringed. They had. Shifting about, but avoiding Ransom's gaze, she mumbled, "Yes—I mean no. I'm all right." Why had Isaac's question flustered her? Maybe because the thought that a wealthy man like Ransom Shepard would look twice at an uneducated waitress such as herself had never occurred to her. Isaac was probably being funny again. Apparently the two men loved kidding each other.

She'd turned to escape when she heard Isaac exclaim loudly to his boss. "Your *what?* Mail-order bride?" He sounded incredulous, which caused Sara to bite her lip with apprehension. Ransom was explaining her and her sister's presence on the island. Humiliation scalding her cheeks, she scurried up onto the porch, wanting to get packed and away from Ransom Shepard and this whole mortifying experience as quickly as possible.

She stopped to grab a muddy pair of Lynn's shoes that had been abandoned in a corner. While she tried to figure out a way to knock the dirt off of them, she could again hear Ransom and Isaac talking. They were strolling toward the house.

"Just how old is this mail-order bride of yours?" Isaac asked.

"Sixteen. And if you think what I think you're thinking, you're fired."

"My mind's a blank," Isaac stated, humor tinging his voice. "So I gather the other passenger is Tag. I presume you and your *sixteen*-year-old bride want to be alone."

"You're very funny, Dorf," Ransom muttered. "You'll be the funniest man in the unemployment line."

Isaac laughed. "Okay. I'll quit joshing. But you have to admit, for a man who's gone five years ignoring the fact that there are even women on the planet, it's got to be a little funny that you suddenly have a sixteen-year-old bride and her—what?—twenty-five-year-old sexy sister living with you. I mean, it would be tasty fodder for the office gossips."

Sara swallowed and tucked the shoes under one arm. She didn't care to be trapped on the porch eavesdropping, especially considering Isaac's flattery. As quietly as she could, she edged toward the door that led into the house.

"None of this will get back to the office gossips," Ransom decreed from just beyond the porch. "They're both going home. The sixteen-year-old needs a good spanking, and her sister needs . . ."

After a long pause, Isaac asked, "What? What does the older sister need, boss?"

Sara turned the knob soundlessly, her escape a breath away. But for some reason she waited. What did Ransom Shepard think she needed? Why did she even care about his opinion?

The silence stretched to the breaking point. Sara wished she could see Ransom's expression. Was it thoughtful? Was he shrugging indifferently? Was he leering and elbowing his lawyer friend with a lewd wink?

"She needs a ride home," Ransom said finally, his voice hardly discernable above the moaning of the wind.

"Are you sure that's what she needs, or is it what you believe *you* need?" Isaac asked, his voice devoid of humor. "If you want my opinion, I think it's time you had some softness, some sweetness in your life. I know, I know," he objected, as though Ransom had tried to interrupt. "You keep insisting you're too busy, but, boss, no man, not even you, can live by raking in millions alone. You need a woman."

The scrape of a foot ascending a step made Sara jump. As she slipped inside the house, she heard Ransom growl, "Put a cork in it, Dorf. We have papers to sign."

Sara barely made it through the living room, vaulting trash as she went, before the men came inside. She halted just inside the hallway to catch her breath and slow her erratic breathing. Then she realized too late, that she would have to cross in front of the doorway to make a clean escape to her bedroom. Mouthing a word she usually saved for when she stubbed her toe, she could do little more than press herself against the wall and hope Ransom and Isaac weren't aware she was lurking only a few feet away. As she plastered herself there, she heard Isaac exclaim, "What in blazes happened here? Good grief, Rance, this place looks like—"

"Shut up," Rance barked in a sharp whisper, "or I'll be forced—"

"I know, you'll fire me," Isaac retorted. Sara heard a noise that sounded as though someone stumbled. Isaac yelped and in a strangled voice asked, "What's this on the couch? Damned livestock? What the hell are farm animals doing in—"

"They're reindeer, city boy. Hasn't ten years of living away from New York taught you anything?"

"Reindeer?" Isaac asked. "Oh, 'course. Everybody needs a couple of reindeer on the sofa. Where do you keep the elephants? I prefer mine on furniture with a southern exposure."

"Open the blasted briefcase before I cram it into your big mouth," Ransom muttered. "Tag's in the kitchen."

"Doesn't Tag know you have farm animals in the parlor?"

"They're still reindeer. And I'm not in the mood for your jokes right now."

Sara frowned, listening closely. So Isaac wasn't used to seeing Ransom's home resemble a city dump. She began to actually believe Ransom *was* working some crazy sort of psychological scam on the kids. Crazy, unique—but far from successful.

Isaac made a false start, as if he wanted to complain but apparently thought better of it. Sara could picture Ransom scowling the man down, and she felt for the lawyer. She'd been backed into a corner by the intimidating force of Ransom's scowl more than once.

"What about those contracts?" Ransom asked, his tone rich with unspoken warning.

Sara listened. Hearing papers being shuffled, she dared to peek around the corner. Both men were bent over a briefcase, which balanced precariously on the mess that littered the coffee table. Now was her chance to get to the bedroom. With a deep breath bolstering her courage, she crept by, making a good escape.

Five minutes later, she'd packed one of Lynn's bags with her own belongings and had started throwing Lynn's things into the other suitcase her sister had brought. It would have been impossible to fold anything, even if she had time and her fingers were working properly. Lynn's clothes were too wrinkled and hoplessly jumbled.

Sara was anxious to be away, but there was a tiny part of her that was upset by this abrupt leave-taking. No, she decided, as she stuffed the muddy shoes in with Lynn's other soiled belongings, it wasn't so much the sudden departure as the way Ransom had put it. He'd ordered her off the island. It was all too clear how determined he was to be rid of the troublesome Eller sisters.

As she pressed down on the lid of the battered suitcase and struggled to fasten it, she muttered, "This is absolutely fine, Mr. Eleven-million-dollar-deal. I'm tickled pink to be leaving! You needn't have ordered me to go! I wouldn't stay here with you if you begged, not if you pleaded, not for the whole eleven million!"

"Did you say something to me, Miss Eller?"

Sara's head snapped up. Ransom was lounging in the doorway, his expression narrowed and unreadable. "Something about begging and pleading?"

Annoyed that he'd overheard, she shot him a withering glance and fibbed, "I was just trying to recall a country-and-western song, er, about..."

"Begging and pleading?" he repeated.

"Whatever," she mumbled in a grudging voice. "What do you want?"

"Tag went to get Lynn." He folded his arms across his chest. "She'll be here to help in a minute."

"I'm nearly done. No problem." Not sure why, she stood up to face him. "If you ever decide to quit bird-watching as a hobby, you could try eavesdropping. You should put a use to that stealthy way you have of catching people unawares."

"If I might make a suggestion?" he asked, allowing her insult to go unchallenged. "Don't do so much for Lynn. She won't appreciate you for it."

"Oh?" she countered, her tone clipped. "And I suppose you know all the answers, Mr. Reverse Psychology! If you'll excuse me, I need to get our toilet articles from the bathroom."

His pewter gaze was powerful and difficult to ignore as it roamed speculatively over her. After an unnerving moment, he stepped aside. Without a word, he left her standing there, her throat scratchy dry and her hands clenched at her side in little white balls of fury.

How could he rattle her so badly with a few words and a disturbing glance? No man had ever affected her like this before—somehow short-circuiting her good sense and her free will. Stalking to the bathroom, she snatched up her toothbrush, toothpaste and soap container, grumbling, "Good riddance, Mr. Ransom Shepard. Good, fine, *wonderful* riddance!"

A few minutes later, a suitcase in each hand, she reentered the living room. She stood hesitantly by the doorway, unwilling to interrupt the two men. Ransom was asking Isaac, "How's everything else going?"

The lawyer bent to close the case. "As well as can be expected without our great leader."

"Good."

"Do I dare inquire how everything's going here?" the lawyer asked when he'd straightened, his features perplexed. "If your mood and the condition of this place are any indication, I'd guess somebody needs his big hard head examined."

"Things are on schedule," Ransom said. Sara watched him take Isaac by his expensively suited arm and haul him toward the front door.

"On schedule?" Isaac said. "You call this on schedule? Thank heavens you're not *ahead* of schedule, or this house would be rubble."

Ransom grunted. "If you ever decide to give up being my lawyer, you could starve as a stand-up comic."

"No fooling, Rance," Isaac protested, as they reached the door. "What's going on?"

Sara noticed the sudden sobering of Ransom's manner as he responded, "You know why I'm here. I'm doing the best I know how."

Isaac placed a friendly hand on Ransom's shoulder. "I also know how tough this whole thing's been on you since your wife—"

"I'm not in the mood to reminisce, if you don't mind."

Isaac dropped his hand, looking agitated. "Buddy, from where I stand, you're not in much of a mood at all. Is there something else bothering you besides Tag's—"

"Okay, we're ready," Sara interjected, deciding she'd better announce herself. But she was curious about Ransom's wife and wondered what Isaac had been about to say. It was none of her business, though, and she decided it was best not to pry.

Ransom turned to see her there, his expression guarded. "You're rather stealthy yourself, Miss Eller. I didn't hear you come in."

Her cheeks drained of color at his rebuke, but she didn't have time to speak. Isaac rushed forward to take her bags. "Those look pretty hefty for a little thing like you," he said.

She graced the lawyer with a friendly smile. He was nice and she liked him, in spite of his relationship with Ransom. "Why, thank you, Mr. Dorfman."

"Call me Isaac—"

"Dorf will take you and Lynn back to Anchorage," Ransom interrupted gruffly. Then, addressing Isaac, he added, "Get them on the first plane to Kansas."

"Be my pleasure," Isaac said, beaming like a schoolboy as he readjusted the bags and hoisted his briefcase under his arm.

"I think you'd better get going," Ransom reminded them, his tone chilly.

Sara forced herself to meet his gaze. "Where's Lynn?"

"Outside, prolonging her goodbyes to Boo and Baby."

"Oh!" Sara said, having a sudden thought. "I forgot my overnight case."

She hurried down the hall to her bedroom. When she came back, everyone had gone outside. She frowned at the open door. It was distressingly clear that Ransom would shoot them out of a cannon to get them off the island—any method that was quick and permanent. With determined strides, she, too, departed the house. Fixing her gaze beyond Ransom's shoulder, she called, "Goodbye Tag. Write often."

"I will," he groused, obviously unhappy to see Lynn go.

The children hugged each other while Sara steadfastly refused to look in Ransom's direction. Her pride was injured, and she knew her stubborn chin was stuck out defiantly, but she couldn't help herself. Why she felt slapped in the face by his desire to be rid of them was beyond her. Didn't she want to leave as much as he wanted her to go?

Lynn whined pathetically, "Do I have to go, Rance?"

Against her will, Sara scanned his profile, then hurriedly glanced away again. His mouth was tight and grim, yet it was still the most handsome mouth she could recall seeing on any man. He seemed irritated, too. Why? He was getting exactly what he wanted.

"You can't stay here, Lynn," Ransom explained quietly, drawing Sara's unwilling gaze, "Your sister is your family."

Lynn shot Sara a peevish look, then declared to Ransom, "She's my jailer. I want to stay here with you and Tag."

A shadow of annoyance darkened his features for an instant, but he said only, "Nobody gets everything they want, Lynn. Nobody." In a surprise move, he shifted to face Sara. After a long, quiet perusal, the beginnings of a smile touched the corners of his mouth. "As for you, Miss Eller, I still like your hair."

Sara's mouth gaped in shock. He couldn't resist one parting shot. With a rebellious toss of her head, she said coolly, "Well, that happy news certainly makes this whole trip worthwhile. By the way," she added, her lips thinning with anxiety, "I'll pay you back for what our tickets cost you. Every cent."

"You don't have the money. Forget it."

His response, though spoken gently, held a note of impatience that grated on Sara. She swallowed hard and met his stern expression, repeating, "You'll get every cent."

His stare drilled into her. Theirs was a war of two strong wills, but Sara could see in the stubborness of those hooded eyes that he would never allow her to pay him back. Knowing she had lost, she still insisted tightly, "I'll send the money in payments."

His twisted smile told her she could send him checks from now until halibut flew, and he wouldn't cash them. "Goodbye Miss Eller, Lynn." He nodded curtly to the sisters. Then, with a meaningful frown at Isaac, he abruptly dismissed them, remarking, "Don't screw up this eleven-million-dollar deal, Dorf, or—"

"I know, I'll be the best-dressed ex-corporate-lawyer-stand-up-comic in the unemployment line." He grinned, but it looked forced. Sara knew the tense exchange she'd had with Ransom must have made him uncomfortable. Her heart went out to him.

Not bothering to smile, Ransom said, "You'd better go."

Isaac glanced at his boss speculatively, then murmured, "I'll take care of everything."

"Dad," Tag said, putting an arm about Lynn's shoulders. "I'm going to the plane to see them off."

Ransom's nod was brief as he turned his back to Sara.

It was apparent that Ransom intended to avoid any further eye contact. Not caring to prolong their awkward, frosty departure, Sara whirled away and set off toward the island's airstrip. There was, after all, nothing more to say.

SARA STOOD ON THE GROUND waving as Isaac's plane left the runway, feeling a knot forming in her stomach. She resisted the urge to scream out her frustration, but just barely. As the plane winged its way toward the clouds, Sara watched her chance of escaping this nightmare slip from her grasp. Because of some silly rule about weight and fuel consumption or some such aviation nonsense, Isaac's pilot had been adamant that he could only take on one additional passenger. What was Sara to do? She couldn't go off and leave Lynn—not and be sure she'd ever see her wayward sister again.

Nor could she stay and send Lynn back by herself. She didn't even know if they still had an apartment, since this trip had made it impossible to pay this month's rent. She didn't know if old Mrs. Hermly would give her extra time to pay, and she didn't want Lynn wandering the streets, homeless. Darn that antiquated satellite station! Why did it have to be out? How did these people live without phones?

Of course Isaac had been sorry he had to leave them. But he'd had to go. As he'd said, if he didn't there would be eleven million dollars' worth of hell to pay. She could understand that. Nobody in their right mind would willingly throw away that much money. So, there'd been no choice but for both Sara and Lynn to remain behind.

As the threesome approached Ransom's house, the teenagers sped on ahead, laughing and whooping, excited by their reprieve.

Suspecting Ransom would be working at the nearest bird cliff, Sara decided not to put off the inevitable. She might as well confront him with the bad news. It would be better to do battle out of earshot of the children, who'd bounded inside the house.

Trudging along the cliff's edge, she finally saw him. He was just standing there, his legs braced wide, his hands on his hips, staring out to sea. He didn't appear to be watching birds anymore. It looked as though he was lost in thought, staring off in the direction the plane had disappeared. Long gone from view, he was still peering after it. Probably offering a silent good-riddance speech, Sara groused inwardly. Well, it didn't matter what he thought. They were stuck together for a while longer whether he liked it or not. She'd faced it—now it was his turn.

The shrill *kitti-waaake, kitti-waaake* of a gray-and-white kittiwake swooping low made her jump as she neared Ransom's imposing back. She realized how overwrought she'd become in anticipation of their impending quarrel, and she gulped to ease the tension in her prickly throat.

How would he react, she wondered? Would he rant and rave, or would he shrug, grin in that doesn't-bother-me way, and say, "Whatever." She couldn't decide which would upset her more, his anger or his indifference.

"Mr. Shepard?" she tried, but her voice completely failed her. Clearing her throat, she tried again, this time breaking through his reverie. He twisted around abruptly, as though he'd recognized her voice and couldn't believe his ears.

She bit her lower lip and looked away, carefully avoiding his antagonistic eyes.

"What the hell . . . ?" he asked in a rough-edged whisper.

She lifted her chin, daring him to shout. "I don't like this any better than you do. But it seems there are rules about how many people can ride in small airplanes—something about fuel and wind and weight."

He stared, wordless, for so long that her morbid curiosity got the better of her and she faced him. His dark expression was unreadable.

"Well, don't you have anything to say?" she challenged, not quite successful in her bid for nonchalance.

His lips lifted in a scornful grin, and she caught her breath at its devilish beauty.

"So, you and your sister exceeded the plane's weight allowance," he said, contrary amusement glimmering in his eyes. "Eat a lot of pork back there in Kansas, do you?"

She reddened. Sarcasm! So that was the route he'd decided to take. Refusing to let him bait her, she retorted, "Have you ever thought of going to blazes?"

He sobered then. It was as if someone had flipped off a switch, killing the light in his eyes. They'd gone a leaden gray. His gaze veered back toward the sea, and he curled his hands into fists.

Sara had the oddest feeling that if he'd responded to her remark, he would have said, "I've been there." The expression she'd seen on his face was almost haunted.

A stab of regret slashed her heart. She'd opened a painful wound out of his past. He was still grieving for his wife; the loss of a spouse was a hellish torture for anyone. Staring morosely at his rigid shoulders, she murmured, "That was insensitive of me. But in my own defense, Mr. Shepard, your insults are hard to ignore."

After what seemed like an hour of strained silence, he shook his head, conceding flatly, "You're right. I give you a lot of trouble, Miss Eller. I'm the one who should apologize." He turned back, and their eyes met. The depth of the remorse in his gaze struck her like a blow. To her shock, she saw something else in those storm-ridden eyes, something she could only describe as desire, and she shivered with reaction.

Could it be that Ransom Shepard was as attracted to her as she was to him? Could it be that he was fighting that attraction with every verbal and physical weapon he had, just as she had been fighting it? She toyed with her zipper hasp, carefully avoiding his eyes.

"Forget it, Mr. Shepard," she said, trying to sound unaffected. "It won't be long now, anyway, before you're rid of us. Isaac said he'd do everything in his power to help."

"He said he'd send the plane back?" Ransom asked very quietly, drawing her regard.

"Not exactly." She shivered again, not sure if the involuntary motion was still in reaction to what she'd thought she'd seen in his eyes, or from the chill of the sea spray. One thing was clear, though—it was entirely too cold and damp for her light jacket. "But I'm sure he'll send the plane back. Aren't you?"

One corner of Ransom's mouth lifted, but there was no merriment in his expression. "I'm afraid not," Ransom murmured. "He's got a twisted sense of loyalty. He said he was going to help, not send the plane back."

She was confused. "What do you mean?"

Ransom surprised her by taking her arm. "Let's go inside. I can hardly hear you for the chattering of your teeth."

"But what do you mean, a twisted sense of loyalty?" she repeated, trying to keep from stammering.

He chuckled, but it had a harsh edge. "A little while ago, Dorfman told me I needed a woman," he explained grimly. "I think he's chosen you as a likely candidate."

"Me?" She stumbled to a halt, staring at him. "I hope you don't mean he expects us to...to..."

"I imagine that's exactly what he expects."

His revelation couldn't have been more amazing. Her lips trembled and a little gasp escaped her throat.

"The idea is appealing to you, I can see," he replied with heavy irony. "You pallor is quite an ego-builder, Miss Eller. I'm flattered."

She stared at him, at a loss for words.

"Our sleeping together was Dorfman's idea, not mine," he reminded her.

Outraged, she used all her waning strength to yank her arm from his grasp, and she staggered backward. Even though she'd overheard Isaac say he thought Ransom needed a woman, she refused to believe he would concoct such a sordid plan involving her. Mortified and hurt, she declared, "That plane will be back!"

One dark brow rose. "Would you care to make a little wager?"

"How much?"

"Ten thousand dollars."

She gaped at him, condemning his audacity with her stare. Finally finding her voice, she muttered, "Don't be ridiculous."

He surveyed her with a penetrating regard, but said nothing else. Deciding to rush to the offensive and change the subject, she shot back, "I warn you, Mr. Shepard, if you ever try to lay one lustful finger on me, you'll be sorry. I took a self-defense class, and I know how to hurt you." With that she pivoted away from him and tromped off toward the house.

A moment later she felt a strong grip on her elbow, causing her to stumble toward her captor. A muscle twitched in his jaw, betraying his foul mood. "I'm sure you could do me damage, Sara. There's no doubt in my mind." He began to drag her toward the house again. Jaws clenched, he added, "I hope you don't mind my calling you Sara."

She stiffened. "I mind! I mind everything you've said and done since I got here!"

"Fine," he replied, his indifference almost palpable. "And while we wait for that plane, you may call me Rance."

CHAPTER FIVE

RANSOM HAULED his red-haired captive along, his anger far from concealed, and Sara winced at the fire that smoldered in his eyes.

"By heaven!" he growled. "I'm going to throttle Dorfman the next time I get my hands on the man."

"You can't know for sure he won't send the plane back," Sara objected breathlessly.

Ransom hissed a curse between his teeth and Sara's eyes widened in apprehension.

"Don't I? Well, the last time I checked, the company plane comfortably held six passengers. My matchmaking lawyer put the pilot up to telling you that garbage about weight allowance. Mark my words—Isaac wants me to have a woman, pure and simple, and he thinks a lovely redhead like you is a good candidate."

Sara stared at his angular profile, her cheeks hot with stunned embarrassment. He'd called her a lovely redhead. She tried not to be affected by the compliment—after all, the words had been spoken more as a bitter complaint than a tribute—but she failed.

Ransom bit off another curse, and Sara flinched. She wondered if this was how innocent people felt before they were going to hang for a crime they didn't commit. Just when she thought he was going to fling her to the ground and grab a strong piece of rope, he loosened his hold and slowed his pace, as though he'd realized she was too small to keep up with his breakneck jog.

When they reached the porch, he let her go. She whirled to face him, accusing breathlessly, "I've never been so cruelly manhandled by..." Struggling for air, she stopped to inhale deeply.

He crossed his arms on his chest. "A man?" he queried angrily, then expelling a slow breath, his expression grew contrite. "Blast it—forgive me, Sara. I suppose I don't react very well when I've been hoodwinked."

"I didn't hoodwink you," she reminded him. "And I don't see how you can be so sure the plane won't be back. Maybe they had lots of baggage on the plane that made it heavy or something. I refuse to believe he lied."

"The next time I see Dorfman, I'll kill him," Ransom muttered wearily. "Then I'll fire him."

"He knew you'd say that," she retorted, frowning at the memory. "When he had to leave, er, left without us. His exact words were, 'I'll be the best-dressed ex-corporate-lawyer-stand-up-comic-dead-man in the employment line.'"

A flicker of surprise softened Ransom's stern stare. Then a smile gradually blossomed on his face, appearing almost authentic. After a long, slow shake of his head, he startled Sara with a chuckle that built into genuine laughter.

The sound was deeper and more hearty than the crash of waves breaking on the beach. Sara could only stand there, feeling the warmth of his unexpected good humor enter her chilled bones. His capacity to exude such a tangible appeal stunned her. No man had ever affected her in this alarming way before—especially a man she detested. It was as though his strength of will had invaded her being, wrapping itself about her core, stealing some piece of herself.

"Why is that so funny?" she asked, her voice fragile as she pushed back such absurd notions.

Amused exasperation sparked in his eyes. "I can never stay mad at that guy."

She sniffed in disbelief. "Is that why you fire him every fifteen minutes?"

Ransom's tone became affectionate. "Isaac's a good man, a good friend. His intentions are the best, however misguided. He's more like a brother to me than—" He cut himself off, and his features hardened. Sara was jolted to see tears in his eyes. He blinked and then grinned, all evidence of anguish gone. "Let's just say ol' Dorf's job is safe."

Sara was so unnerved by what she'd glimpsed—some rending sadness within Ransom—that she couldn't speak or move. He'd covered the slip quickly enough, but she couldn't help wondering what he'd been about to reveal. Bolstering her courage, she prompted, "Isaac's more a brother to you than who? Do you have a brother?"

His handsome mouth thinned, and when he spoke his words were low and razor sharp. "No, Sara, I have no brother." Turning on his heel, he stalked into the house.

THE NEXT DAY DAWNED sunny and what might even pass for warm. The temperature hovered around fifty. A gentle breeze caressed the landscape, and Sara found the feel of sunshine on her face a welcome change. The kids had gone down to the cove to play with their dolphin friend, Potluck, and Sara, having walked miles and miles already, was back at the house burning with a need to do something constructive. Against her will, she was caught in the throes of another attack of I-have-to-clean-this-place-or-I'll-scream.

Ransom, making his regular round of observations at his plotted bird cliffs, would probably be gone for some time. Sara decided to take her life into her hands and search for a vacuum cleaner. She'd unobtrusively been clearing a path for the past two days, and today, she decided she would vacuum that path, no matter who disapproved of the idea. Of course, there were those who would say she was being a coward by cleaning up while no one was there to object. But those busybodies would be wrong. She would eventually have to face Ransom's towering condemnation. At least, when that happened, there'd be a vacuumed path to aid in her escape.

After twenty minutes, Sara grew nervous. She'd wasted precious time searching the house, and the vacuum cleaner was nowhere to be found. It had to be in Ransom's closet. She hated to venture into his room. It seemed like an invasion of privacy, though he didn't keep his door closed during the day. She'd glimpsed inside several times and discovered that it was every bit as debris-strewn as the rest of the house. Even so, she felt a twinge of guilt as she entered.

Guilt increasing her heart rate, she looked around and saw what once had been a nice room. The furniture was made of mellow old wood that was practical and hospitable. There was a black, brass-studded trunk at the foot of the unmade bed. A biscuit-colored area rug was littered with clothes, as was a long bench that sat beneath the wide window facing the sea. A black-framed portrait above the bed was of Ransom and the same woman Sara had seen in the small silver frame she'd dropped. The woman in the portrait, snuggled next to Ransom, was holding a dark-haired boy of about four. They were all smiling. Sara flushed, aware that it was a photograph of Ransom's family in happier days. Disconcerted by the contented image they presented, she turned away.

The door to the closet was closed. She hurried over and touched the knob with trepidation, not sure why she felt like such a thief. As she turned the knob, the door swung open. A light went on, making her gasp. She got hold of herself. A lot of closet doors were rigged to do that.

Stepping inside, she inspected the deep closet. It was as though she'd walked into another universe—a parallel, but immaculate universe. She gawked. Lynn had been right. Their host did keep a very neat closet.

So, it was true. He was *not* a natural slob. His shoes were lined with military preciseness on several low shelves. Above those shelves were two rods, one over the other. On the top rod, cotton shirts were arranged, short-sleeve in front, long-sleeve behind. On the lower rod, knit shirts were arranged closer to the door, and plaid flannel shirts were hung farther back.

On the other side of the closet pressed slacks and jeans hung like a row of soldiers at attention. Behind them were several sports coats and winter jackets. To the rear of that rod, a set of shelves held stacks of folded sweaters.

An odd feeling came over Sara as she searched the walk-in closet—a feeling of safety. She had no idea why a well-ordered closet had such a comforting effect on her, but it did. Perhaps it was merely the wonderful scent if gave off. Ransom's scent lingered here like a benevolent spirit. She crept over and placed a hand on one of the orderly piles of sweaters. The white one she touched was pure cashmere, and soft as swan's down.

Strange, unbidden tears came to her eyes. Something long forgotten came rushing back to her mind's eye: those halcyon days before her parents died. She remembered playing house in her father's closet before Lynn was born. How tranquil and happy a place it had been.

Though Ransom in no way reminded her of her father, there was something solid and reassuring about his closet. Ransom was a complicated, solitary man, and seeing his closet neat and devoid of clutter solved a small part of the mystery that surrounded him. Yet discovering this detail also did one very important thing to Sara. It made her crave to know Ransom better. No man could keep a closet so pristine, have it exude a feeling of such security, and be the disreputable slob he portrayed himself to be.

She knew there would be those who might argue that this closet represented a compulsive person, but they wouldn't be able to convince Sara of that. Not about Ransom or about her father, who had been neat, too. He'd been a caring man—not only with his wife and daughters, but with his possessions. "Care for them and they'll care for you," he used to say with a gentle smile. That philosophy stood for everything and everyone that had come into contact with her father, and Sara knew intuitively that Ransom was like him in that way. She recalled the portrait she'd seen over his bed. Ransom's arm was looped protectively around his wife and son. If he took this kind of care with mere possessions, how much more care would he lavish on those he loved?

Ransom wasn't the type of man to bandy about details of his grief and worries, so he must have silently, uncomplainingly, endured great sadness and loneliness in his life. Sara was sure that beneath his careless facade, Ransom was a loving, stable man who'd been doing his best to raise his rebellious son. Because of his grief, Ransom had cut himself off from people, from relationships—even his own boy, for five years. Tag had made that clear early on. Ransom had no intention of getting close to anyone—especially a woman. She closed her eyes, feeling sad. But she understood, and she respected his grief. She only wished he trusted her enough to—

"What do you think you're doing?"

She whirled to see Ransom looming at the closet door, staring at her as though she'd tried to pick his pocket and been caught in the act. She swallowed and decided she looked as guilty as she felt.

"I...I was looking for the, um, vacuum..." She allowed the explanation to drift away, not sure what excuse she might use for looking for an instrument of cleanliness, considering the house rules.

He scowled, displeasure hovering in his eyes. "It's in the basement. What do you want it for?"

Miffed at being treated like a child, she said, "I was going to fling it into the sink. I think with a few superfluous cleaning appliances, we could reach the ceiling—probably make the Guiness Book of Records for 'Most Revolting Housekeeping.'"

"You're every bit as entertaining as Dorfman," he replied dryly.

She decided he wasn't going to fly off the handle, so she opted to try for some actual communication. "Ransom," she began, tentatively meeting his eyes. "I...shouldn't have gotten smart with you. It's just that you make me..." She faltered. "What I mean is, I believe you now." Swinging her arm about her, she indicated the small room. "Your closet is so...so different from the rest of the house. I realize now you were telling me the truth about trying reverse psychology on the kids. I, er, owe you an apology."

To her surprise he showed no reaction. Appraising her silently, he said, "You owe me nothing, Sara." Then he walked out of her range of vision, but called back loudly enough for her to hear, "Just don't use that vacuum for anything but getting in Guiness. Is that clear?"

Sara was darned if she was going to allow him to walk away from her again. With resolute strides, she caught up to him as he entered the living room and demanded to his back, "Don't you think we should try another tack now? I mean your psychology idea is failing. The house is a wreck."

He didn't turn but kept going toward the front door as he observed. "Thank you for that encouraging input."

"So you're not going to discuss it at all?" she complained, frustrated.

"You've got it."

"And to think I apologized to you!" she cried in exasperation. "Ransom Shepard, haven't you ever heard of the fine art of communication?"

"I've heard of it, Sara," he said. "The problem is, you can't seem to accept what I communicate."

The door slammed and he was gone.

THIRTY MINUTES LATER, Sara was calmer as she stood on the ragged edge of a cliff, the salt air in her face. The rocky ledges below were alive with birds either building nests or warming eggs. She'd learned the names of some of the species from Tag. There was a mob of black-and-white, penguinlike murres, sea gulls, parakeet auklets, red-legged kittiwakes and numerous pairs of puffins, with their black backs, white stomaches, bright orange bills and jaunty white tufts of feathers that curled away from white faces over the black crown of their heads. To Sara's untrained eye, they looked very much like parrots.

The air was filled with sound, from the sea pounding the shore a hundred feet below, to the calling, cooing, screaming and crying of the birds as some flew about gathering nesting material and others rested on the precarious ledges below.

She sat down, curling her legs beneath her. As she enjoyed nature's operetta, she toyed with a delicate crimson flower. This island was a magnificent place—full of life that raged and bellowed and frisked about at a frantic pace. Vigor seemed to be the watchword of the Pribilof Islands, as though anything or anyone who attempted to live here had to have substance, energy and possess a great strength of will. No hothouse flowers could survive on this out-of-the way, windswept isle.

Ransom's stalwart form materialized forcefully in her mind—devilishly handsome and carrying himself with a commanding air. Shaken by the unexpected intrusion, she jerked the flower up, roots and all, and held it to her nose, sniffing, trying to push his image away. The flower's scent was bold and haunting, very much like the man she was trying to forget.

She made a face. Ransom again! Why must everything from the flight of birds to the scent of flowers bring him to mind? "Drat it!" she cursed aloud. "I hate you, you bullying troglodyte!"

"Why do I have the feeling you're not referring to Geraldo Rivera?" a deep, amused voice asked at her back.

She twisted around to see the very man she'd been cursing. He stood as she'd often seen him, with his legs braced apart, his arms crossed over his chest. That self-assured stance emphasized the power of his thighs and the slimness of his hips, and she wondered if he knew how physically exciting he was.

His eyes danced with humor. He did know the scoundrel. "What do you mean by sneaking up on me like that?" she demanded in a strangled whisper.

"I was going to offer you a penny for your thoughts, but I've changed my mind. I'm no masochist," he remarked good-humoredly, as though her question hadn't been dipped in venom.

She glared at him warily. "Why are you suddenly in such a good mood?"

"Life's too short. I decided to accept your apology."

Both excited and annoyed by his sudden appearance, Sara tried to show neither emotion, sniffing disinterestedly. "I've been holding my breath, waiting for your forgiveness." Turning away, she pulled her legs up and hugged her knees protectively. She would ignore him *and* his muscled thighs *and* his trim hips *and* his wide chest.

To her surprise, he sat down beside her. It took all her willpower not to glance in his direction. She tried to concentrate on one particular puffin as it swooped and glided across the sky.

"So," he began conversationally, "fancy meeting you here."

She stared straight ahead, keeping her breathing very slow, very calm—at least outwardly. His arm had brushed hers when he sat down. The tingling rush brought on by that light contact was still playing havoc with her equilibrium.

"I was pretty short with you earlier," he said quietly.

It was hard not to look at him, hard not to comment, especially since he seemed to be willing to talk—really talk.

Cautiously she peeked in his direction. "Yes, you were," she agreed.

A slow smile curved his lips. "What if *I* apologize?"

She frowned, fighting the sensuality he exuded. "I didn't think you cared about my opinion."

His compelling eyes narrowed, holding her gaze for a moment before he broke the contact and squinted out to sea. "I'm trying not to."

She watched his profile. His strong features, bronzed by wind and sun, spoke of vitality and timeless strength—very like his island. Hardly able to coax her voice above a whisper, she asked, "Why are you trying not to?"

He surveyed the vastness of the restless water, but seemed to notice nothing in particular. "I have my reasons," he said in an odd tone. The set of his wide shoulders had always spoken loudly of confidence. At this moment, those shoulders seemed to slump slightly.

Sara waited for a long time, but the continued silence began to wear on her nerves. She couldn't bring herself to ask him why he didn't want to care about her opinion, and she couldn't understand her hesitancy. Why was she afraid of the answer? Casting that idea aside, she said, "You're a very private man, aren't you?"

Without looking at her, he replied, "I suppose you consider that a character flaw."

"No, of course not."

"I told you once—my story isn't very interesting."

"I'm interested," she whispered, speaking not with thought, but with feeling.

When he turned back to regard her, she noticed that the breeze had brushed a strand of wavy hair across his brow. She had a mad impulse to smooth it back or to muss it further. She didn't know which desire was stronger, and she tried not to allow herself to dwell on it.

Boldly handsome, he continued to gaze at her. Chewing on the inside of her cheek, she bided her time until he chose to speak. She dared not even breathe for fear he would change his mind and stalk away as he'd done so many times before.

"Don't be interested," he cautioned, a flinty warning in his tone.

A flicker of apprehension shot through her. Why did she feel she had to pursue a subject that was clearly off-limits? Nosiness was unlike her. But something about Ransom Shepard brought out desires in Sara she'd never had. She wanted to know about him, about his wife, his grief. Ignoring his ominous signals, she forged on, "You loved your wife a great deal, didn't you?"

For an instant his glance sharpened. He studied her from beneath down-drawn brows for a heartbeat, then stared out to sea again. The waves crashed and broke into a million rainbow-hued spangles time and again before he began to speak. All during the long silence, the tensing of his square jaw had been the only indication of any emotional turmoil. Finally he asked, "Do you read John le Carré?"

Her heart dropped. She'd expected anything but this complete change of subject. Instead of letting her help him, he was making her feel unsophisticated, which, compared to him, she was. Pretending she didn't care that he'd once again shut her out, she quipped sarcastically, "I don't read much fiction, but my landlady subscribes to tons of magazines, so I'm a font of trivial facts. For instance, I just read an article about dogs and why they bark. Would you like to hear about that?"

He grunted, and she thought he might have found her query mildly amusing. "Actually, I was making a point," he said, flicking a glance her way.

"Oh? What was it?"

"Le Carré once wrote, 'Love is whatever you can still betray.'"

Sara was confused. "I'm sure that's very deep, but I'm afraid you've lost me." She leaned toward him. "That's one of the things that drives me crazy about you. You can never simply say yes or no. Why do you always answer a question with a cryptic remark or, worse, another question?"

"Do I do that?" Turning to face her, he shot her a crooked smile, but his eyes gleamed like cool metal. They were closer now—too close—but Sara made no effort to move away, though something told her she should.

"Ransom Shepard, you're terminally sarcastic," she admonished, frustrated by the insolent mask he hid behind. "Why I thought we could actually talk I'll never know."

He remained absolutely motionless for a moment, watching her. "All right, then—yes," he said finally, "I loved my wife." Unnerving Sara with the gruffness of his admission, he went on, "I loved her right up until the day she died. Does that direct answer cheer you up?"

Sara's throat closed, and she suddenly felt very sad. Sad that she'd forced him to dredge up a painful subject, and sad because she really didn't want to hear how deeply he'd cherished his wife. Pulling her lips between her teeth, she scanned the grass at her feet, nodding jerkily. "I—I'm sorry," she whispered after a taut minute. "That was none of my business."

"That's true," he agreed harshly. "Why do you give a damn, anyway?"

She swallowed, shaking her head. Her voice would have betrayed emotions she didn't dare reveal.

"I think I know. I think we both know," he said, his tone relenting slightly. "You're a very attractive woman, Sara. I think you know I've wanted to make love to you ever since we first met."

Her head shot up. This wasn't what she'd expected him to say at all, but it was having an effect.

His manner grew cynical. "You've gone pale. Does the idea of my lovemaking really disgust you so?"

She sat there blankly, her heart pounding, unable to speak. She was afraid her own fantasies about him would be given away by any attempt at a denial.

"To be honest, Sara, I don't want to give a damn about your opinion—or about your body—but I do." His voice seductive and deep, he challenged softly, "And I think, if you're honest with yourself, you'll realize you feel the same way about me."

"I..." The failed sentence came out like a wistful sigh. It was hard to keep her thoughts coherent when she was so near him. His eyes were mesmerizing, his mouth tempting.

As she stared, transfixed, his features suddenly darkened and he muttered, "*Dammit,* Sara..."

The next instant she found herself being kissed, as hands, large, strong and warm pressed her back onto the cool tundra grasses. His weight was deliciously welcome as he slanted across her body, his lips, tender, yet demanding against hers.

She was startled, but unable—no, unwilling—to struggle against what was happening. His palms were cradling her cheeks, his fingers stroking her temples. His mouth held hers fast in a sweet prison overflowing with dizzying sensations completely foreign to Sara.

She'd been kissed before, but not with such finesse, with such depth of passionate understanding. His teeth nipped at her lips, tantalizing, making her ache for more.

Barely aware of her actions, she lifted her arms to encircle his shoulders and sighed against his mouth, opening her lips in shy invitation.

He groaned, clearly delighted with her surrender, and his kiss deepened. Sara's core grew fevered, fairly throbbing with reaction to his shrewd, masterful seduction. This man was a wanton sorcerer. How had he managed to bring her to the brink of ultimate abandon? He'd uttered not a single soft word. Only an angry curse had been on his lips as he'd taken her in his arms and swept her away from her good sense to a dreamworld where she had no business dwelling.

Hadn't she been warned? Hadn't Ransom told her she'd been left behind because he *needed* a woman? What in heaven's name did she think she was doing flat on her back being no more than a long-overdue fling for this man. With a smothered cry, she moved her arms from their possessive hold about him and pressed them feebly against his chest.

"No..." she managed, twisting her face away. "Get off of me!" Her voice was a miserable half moan, half wail. "You men are so predictable! I wish I had a dollar for every sleazy pass I've had made at me. I'd be richer than... than *you!*"

He remained above her, supporting himself on one elbow. His expression was subdued, but there was something unsettling that glistened in his eyes, beckoning her. It was clear he had been affected, too, and didn't want this wild interlude between them to end this way.

"Sara," he whispered hoarsely, covering her hand with his.

In a surge of self-preservation, she pulled from his grasp, struggling to her feet to put much-needed distance between them. As she stumbled backward, the feel of his kiss still sizzling on her lips, she was hit by a horrible truth. She wanted very badly to have this man make love to her. There was something about him that touched her deep inside, something unnameable, risky, considering the fact that he'd so recently admitted he'd loved his wife very deeply and obviously still grieved for her.

Now she understood the reason she'd been unable to ask him why he didn't want to care about her opinion. She'd sensed this coming between them. And with his scandalously lusty kiss, the truth had caught her full force.

"Good-time Sara," she flared breathlessly. "Is that what you want me to be?"

He was frowning now. "It would make things simpler, yes," he muttered.

She recoiled at his bluntness. "And you think...you really believe I'd have made love to you out here on the grass?" she cried, dismayed.

His nostrils flaring with ire, he sat up, yanking a hand through his hair. "I didn't put much thought into it, Sara," he groused. "It just happened. Like lightening, unpredictable and beautiful."

And dangerous! she added silently.

The tensing of his jaw betrayed his frustration. "Damn me," he snarled. "I have to admit, Dorfman was right. I've been without a woman too long." Swearing impatiently, he shifted his gaze to her, his expression critical. "But judging by what happened a minute ago, I'd wager you're not as immune to me as you'd like to think."

She felt a painful catch in her chest and hoped it wasn't because his aim was so accurate. Going quivery and defensive, she charged, "It must be difficult to carry around an ego as unwieldy as yours!"

His eyes grew cold. "It's not ego, Sara. It's the raw truth. You know it, blast it! I wasn't the one giving off 'kiss me' signals."

Her mouth sagged in disbelief. "And to think less than an hour ago I could have sworn you were an honorable man," she hissed, shaking her head in hot denial.

"Even honorable men have needs," he said. "I haven't had a woman in a long time, and I have no soft emotions left to give, but that doesn't exempt me from human needs. So, Sara, if you're not liberated enough to follow through with your come-ons, then stay the hell away from me."

She stared, horrified. She *hadn't* come on to him! "I never..." she protested indignantly.

One dark brow lifted in scorn. "You can lie to me if you must, but don't lie to yourself."

Her face burned with mortification. She knew she'd had thoughts, fantasies of kissing him, of him kissing her, but she'd had no idea she was telegraphing her desires so clearly. Upset, she blurted, "What you're saying..." She had to stop and swallow to calm her voice. "What you're saying is, you think I was *asking* to be kissed? That it was *my* fault?"

With a twisted, contemptuous flash of teeth, he turned toward the ocean, stretching out his long legs before him. "Go home, Sara," he demanded coldly. "Go home before I do something I'll regret."

"What do you want to do? Punch me?"

He cast her a heavy-lidded glance. "I want to make love to you."

She heard herself gasp.

A short, malignant chuckle rumbled deep in his chest. "Don't panic. I won't attack you, Sara. I don't want a relationship, and you don't want to feel used. So, there's no point in starting something we'd both be sorry for."

The fierce bitterness in his voice startled her and she frowned down at him. He was withdrawing from her before her very eyes. Evidently, now that sanity had returned, he was regretting his lapse.

Though the day was relatively mild, Sara was suddenly very cold, and she shivered. Hugging herself, she began to back away. Her stomach clenched. Why? It couldn't be regret that he'd slipped back behind his self-protective mask and become, once again, an aloof enigma.

She should be happy he was ignoring her. Hadn't *she* been the one to demand that they end the kiss? He hadn't rejected her; it had been the other way around. Why, then, did she feel so rejected? Was she going nuts? Her breathing became labored, coming in harsh little pants, and her pulse raced like that of a frightened doe.

Having it end like this was for the best, she told herself. Even if she had given in to his sexual charms, did she really believe he'd make an effort to carry on a long-distance relationship between his salmon factories in Alaska and her apartment in Andover, Kansas?

Not likely!

She tried to reassure herself. *This swift end to any brief, tawdry physical alliance is absolutely the best thing I could have done. Absolutely the best...*

Ransom was scanning the sea, leaning casually back on his elbows, plainly unconcerned that she was lingering nearby. She stood there, stone-still, watching him watch the ocean. After a very short time, the pang of his emotional abandonment became intolerable, and she whirled from him and broke into a run. As she lurched away, she covered her mouth with both hands to staunch the sobs of disappointment and regret she could neither quell nor understand.

CHAPTER SIX

SARA'S HEAD JERKED UP. She thought she heard a strange noise coming from the kitchen. Running water? Curious, she made her way toward the sound.

It was Tuesday morning, and since their kiss on the cliff, Ransom and Sara had coexisted with strained civility. Their eye contact had been brief and hostile, at least on her part. His gunmetal gaze had been impenetrable.

Right now she wasn't sure where he was, but she knew he wasn't in the house. So what was the odd noise coming from the kitchen? If she didn't know better she would have sworn someone was washing dishes.

Rounding the corner, she saw Tag and Lynn hunched together near the sink. Tag was pouring dishwashing detergent into the running torrent, making bubbles mound into the air like clouds, while Lynn thumbed through a book.

"What's going on here?" Sara asked.

They turned as one, both looking deadly serious. Tag shrugged. "We're sick of salmon and beans."

Lynn glanced back down at the book and addressed Tag. "Think we have enough flour for pancakes?"

"We've got tons. Syrup?"

Lynn grimaced and walked to the pantry. Opening it, she poked her head inside, shouting back, "Two big bottles. So it's pancakes and bacon?"

"Sounds good to me. I'll wash the griddle, you find some plates."

Sara stared in awe as Lynn dragged a couple of plates off the counter and slipped them into the sudsy water.

"I'd better get glasses, too," she muttered.

"Right. And forks, maybe knives."

Lynn nodded and began to scrounge silverware and glasses from the messy kitchen.

"Oh, pooh," Lynn groused. "We're gonna need mixing bowls."

"Yeah," Tag agreed reluctantly. "Maybe we'd better just start washing, then worry about what we'll need later."

Lynn gathered up an armload of china, pots and pans and settled them in the sink. Apparently having forgotten that Sara was standing there, the pair went about washing and drying. Sara was glued to the entrance, transfixed as they began to stack dishes on shelves.

She finally managed, "Aren't you going to ask me for help?"

Lynn peered over her shoulder and grumbled, "Yeah, sure. Since when have you helped lately?"

Sara pursed her lips. It was true. She'd followed Ransom's rules, even though it had been against her will. "You have a point." With that, she turned away, hiding a smile. "Enjoy your pancakes."

"No thanks to you," Lynn griped.

Still dazed by the miracle she'd witnessed in the kitchen, Sara took her jacket from the entryway closet and wandered outside. She'd been walking for several minutes before she realized she was actually looking for Ransom. It wasn't because she wanted to see him, she told herself sternly; it was because he should know about the phenomenon taking place inside the house.

As she hiked toward the cliffs where she knew he observed and recorded the goings-on of the island's nesting birds, she began to have a nagging feeling. He'd been right all along. His reverse-psychology ploy was working.

She shook her head incredulously and plunged her hands into her pockets. The man's ulterior motives for his iron-fisted slovenliness had begun to pay off—unless this spate of dishwashing and cooking by the kids was a wild, once-in-a-lifetime fluke. She rather doubted that, though, and hoped for the best.

As Sara trudged on, she noticed that the sky was overcast and rain threatened, but somehow the gloom didn't dampen her spirits as it had when she'd first arrived. These slate-gray heavens enhanced the vivid greens of the tundra and gave a deep, cobalt richness to the ocean. She loved the sunny days, of course, but she'd acquired a fondness for those times when nature cast its somber cloak around the island's ebony cliffs and rolling hills.

She only wished the man of mystery she sought made her feel as welcome as his island. Unfortunately for her peace of mind, he did have the same capacity as his tempestuous isle to make her feel alive, tingling and aware of the fact that she was young and in the full bloom of her womanhood. She shivered with the truth of it. For years she'd hardly noticed that she'd neglected her personal life in favor of caring for her sister. But since his kiss, she felt it with the heaviness of a boulder on her heart. And who was to blame for this discontent, this worrisome self-revelation?

She scanned the horizon and saw him lying on his stomach, the binoculars drawn up to his eyes as he watched the cliffs below his vantagepoint. She stiffened, disturbed by the sight of him.

When she reached his side, she dropped to her knees near the edge of the cliff. "Ransom—"

"Shush," he whispered, with a warning touch on her supporting arm. His scrutiny never left whatever he was observing on some unknown outcropping of rocks below.

She dropped her gaze to see his hand curl about her wrist as he added in a barely audible tone, "Don't break the mood."

She frowned, wanting to ask what mood she could possibly be breaking, but she remained quiet. Her breathing grew shallow and erratic as she tried to ignore the feel of his warm fingers. After a prolonged moment, when he didn't release her, she slipped her arm out of his grasp and silently took deep, calming breaths.

A half minute later, he rolled to his side and looked up at her, his expression serious, but not angry. "What is it?"

She peered over the cliff, finally asking, "What mood?"

One of his dark brows arched. "Have you no romance in you, Sara? This is, after all, mating season."

His meaning came to her like a dash of cold water in the face, and she felt a twinge of embarrassment. Maybe because they'd almost done the same thing on these very cliffs yesterday. "Uh, oh..." she mumbled, then faltered to a halt.

He inclined his head, admonishing, "You wouldn't want to be responsible for a declining kittiwake population, would you?"

She frowned. "Are they endangered?"

Sitting up, he brushed grass from the front of his sweater. "No, but they were having such a good time."

Her cheeks warmed, but she refused to be baited. "Ransom, I came out here to tell you something."

He drew up one leg and encircled his knee with a muscular arm. "All right," he prompted. "Tell me something."

He was inspecting her with those extraordinary eyes, eyes that sparkled with a mixture of peril and enchantment, like silver lightning. For some reason, faced with his intense stare, her brain short-circuited, and she forgot the important information she'd come out here to pass along. At a loss, she opened her mouth a couple of times, but nothing came out.

He smiled mildly. "That's very interesting. You might want to stop and catch your breath."

She jumped to her feet. "I'm sure you think you're hysterically funny, but—"

"Dad?" came a distant call.

Sara turned and saw Tag loping along the open field. By the sound at her back, she could tell Ransom had come to his feet.

When the dark-haired boy reached them, he was panting.

"Problem?" Ransom asked.

Tag shook his head. "Nah. It's just that Lynn and me have some pancakes cooking. We wondered if you'd like some?"

Sara was startled by this uncharacteristic generosity, and she looked at Ransom in order to see his reaction. He appeared calm, but that familiar animosity had come into the depths of his eyes. Pursing his lips, he nodded, "Sounds good. I might have some."

"Ten minutes?" Tag asked.

His father half smiled, but it was more mechanical then genuine. "You've got a deal."

Tag nodded and turned, but before he'd taken a step, he looked back, his expression sheepish. "Dad?" he asked, sounding nervous.

"Yes?"

"What about dinner?"

Ransom shrugged his big shoulders nonchalantly. "What about it?"

"Uh, maybe..." The boy cast his gaze to his feet, and Sara's heart went out to him. Whatever he'd done wrong, he was trying to make amends. She prayed this would be the end of the silent father-son feud. "We—me and Lynn—were thinkin'," Tag went on, "maybe, if we made breakfast, you'd cook us something for dinner."

Sara watched in hopeful anticipation as Ransom considered his son with a wordless frown. Finally, clearing his throat and drawing Tag's skittish gaze, Ransom asked, "When did I ask you to paint the porch?"

The boy seemed to sag. "Three weeks ago."

"Uh-huh," Ransom agreed, nodding. "So, when do you think I might feel like cooking dinner?"

"Three weeks..." Tag allowed the answer to fade away in a listless sigh.

"Sounds about right," Ransom observed. "I look forward to those pancakes. Thanks."

Tag nodded, a picture of dejection. "They're, uh, not very round."

"They'll taste fine," Ransom offered more gently.

Tag started to turn away, then again seemed to have a thought. Screwing up his face as though he had something difficult to ask, he said, "What if I paint it after breakfast?"

"Only if you want to," Ransom commented with little interest.

"I do, I guess. We've been washing dishes, and Lynn's gonna do some laundry."

Ransom's brows lifted in mild surprise. "Oh? Why?"

Tag shook his head. "Well, you and Sara won't let us use your clean towels, and we're all out of underwear. Gee, Dad, we're not animals. We don't want to stink, ya know!"

A flash of wry amusement flitted across Ransom's lips. "Now there's a news bulletin." Gesturing toward the house, he suggested, "You'd better get back and watch those pancakes. Sara and I are getting hungry." He graced Sara with a glance. "Aren't we."

She was startled to be included in the conversation. A second passed before she realized she was expected to answer. Disjointedly she rasped, "Uh, um, yes."

Tag thrust his chin up jerkily, his expression still downcast. "See ya, later."

The boy began walking, but was halted by his father's voice. "Say, Tag, for some reason I just got an urge to cook dinner. Would you rather have barbecued chicken or broiled halibut steaks?"

The youngster swung back around, his green eyes wide with surprise and delight. "Barbecued chicken."

Ransom smiled. "Okay, fine."

With that decided, Tag headed off. Sara watched him gallop over a low rise before she faced her host again. When she did, she was surprised to see that he was watching her. There was a suspicious quirk at the corners of his mouth. "Is that what you wanted to tell me?" he asked.

She nodded mutely.

A bright sparkle of humor at her expense invaded his eyes. "Thanks for the news." Moving past her, he began strolling away.

She detected smugness in his tone and frowned. Aware that he was leaving, she hurried to catch up with him and admitted, "Okay, so you were right and I was wrong. I hope you're happy."

"Happiness is a relative thing."

Exasperated by a week of this man's cryptic remarks, she cried, "What does it take to make you happy?"

"Are you writing my biography, Sara?" he asked evenly.

"You don't trust anybody, do you?"

He shifted to face her, his features hardening. "You're very close." His words, though quiet, were menacing. "But you're not quite on the mark."

"Look, I admit I don't know everything about your situation, but I know there's something wrong between you and Tag, and I'd like to help if you'll let me," she persisted, her voice rising with her frustration. "*Talk* to me!"

"You're right, Sara. You don't know my situation." His manner distant, he cautioned, "Stay out of it." Indicating the direction of the house, he reminded, "Those pancakes will be ready soon. We'd better go."

As he tramped away from her, so tall and remote, Sara stared after him in complete bafflement. He simply refused to allow her any slack at all—no trust, hardly even civility. That was tough to take, especially after the flash of genuine warmth he'd revealed Sunday when he'd pressed her back onto the earth and kissed her.

With great effort, she shook off the giddy feeling the memory brought flooding back, vowing she would not let herself dwell on things that might have been. The incident was behind her—a foolish moment that fortunately hadn't gone too far.

But now she found herself in the difficult position of struggling to be indifferent to Ransom while unexpectedly being filled with a grudging admiration for him. He'd managed to get the kids to do things voluntarily that she hadn't been able to get Lynn to do in years of shouting and threats. She shook her head, at a loss.

EIGHT HOURS LATER, Sara was still reeling from the change that had come over the children. It appeared that the time without clean clothes, dishes or variety in meals had created a craving for order. The inside porch walls were gleaming with a new coat of white paint, and the blue-tile floor in the kitchen had been mopped to a sparkling glimmer. The clutter was gone, and the whole house smelled of pine cleanser.

The place wasn't ready for the cover of *Disinfected Dwellings Gazette,* but the chaos was vastly improved. It was clear to Sara that Lynn and Tag would have done almost anything for barbecued chicken. If she'd only known that years ago. Unfortunately, in Andover, Kansas, there was always a chicken take-out place or a pizza parlor, so no child was ever forced to eat out of cans if she had a couple of dollars. Here, though, there was no choice. It was either cook or starve.

Sara smiled inwardly as Lynn trudged by with another load of dirty clothes. "How's it going?" she asked.

"Fine," Lynn groused, but Sara could tell from the tone of her sister's voice and the lightness of her step that she was not as angry about this tidy turn of events as she let on.

"I thought I'd make peanut-butter pie for dessert," she called, knowing Lynn loved Sara's recipe.

The girl spun around dropping a shower of odd socks in her excitement. "Really? Would you?"

Sara smiled. "Sure. It's been a while."

Lynn grinned. "Wow. Barbecued chicken and peanut-butter pie. I'm so happy I could kiss a skunk."

Sara shook her head at the horrible image Lynn's remark evoked, but she couldn't help laughing. Her laughter sounded strange to her ear, and she wondered how long it had been since she'd had a good laugh.

After a moment, she realized Lynn was laughing, too. Sara watched her sister double over with it. What Lynn had said hadn't been that funny, but they were both laughing hysterically. Maybe it had something to do with the fact that they'd finally learned to appreciate each other a little more. Lynn had learned that she'd taken Sara for granted. And Sara... What, exactly had she learned? It was in there, deep inside her subconscious. All she had to do was dig it out.

Perhaps it was the simple truth that she'd been too protective of Lynn. Looking at her younger sister now, dragging a big load of clothes toward the washer, she realized that, being human, Lynn appreciated a little freedom. Sooner or later, if left to her own devices, she naturally would've reverted from the disgusting slob she'd been to a civilized human being.

Right now, Sara was facing a Lynn Eller who was much more mature than the pouty, defiant high school girl she'd known a week ago. It was a minor miracle.

She also had another thought, a flicker of recognition, that she didn't like, but knew she must consider. Perhaps the nursing career she'd been so fervently saving for hadn't been Lynn's dream, after all. Quite possibly it had been only *her* dream all along. She'd never actually asked Lynn what she wanted to do. Of course, Lynn was young. What did she know?

A noise at the door caught her attention, and she turned wiping impetuous tears from her eyes. The sight of Ransom standing there, backlit by the sun, made her breath catch in her throat. When he took a few steps into the room, Sara could see that his lips were parted in a dazzling display of perfect white teeth. His smiling eyes seemed even more compelling and magnetic. "What's going on here?" he asked.

Lynn filled the breach with a giggly, "I said I was so happy I could kiss a skunk. And it struck Sara funny."

Ransom's gaze moved from Lynn to Sara, his eyes sweeping over her approvingly. "I never suspected you were a devotee of skunk humor."

Her smile faded a little under his warm inspection. "I, er, can take it or leave it, I suppose..." she mumbled, oddly tongue-tied.

"Sara's going to make us peanut-butter pie," Lynn inserted. "You haven't lived till you've tasted her peanut-butter pie."

Ransom considered Sara with eyes gone breathtakingly serious. "Well," he murmured quietly, "apparently my life begins tonight."

FOG, LIKE A SHROUDED demon, held St. Catherine Island in its clammy grip all day Wednesday. Sara made her way out to the rose-colored volcanic-rock airstrip, hoping against hope that old Krukoff's plane would somehow miraculously make it through. But ignoring the old postal-service motto, Krukoff did not deliver in rain or sleet or snow—or cursed, darned, rotten fog!

What was she going to do? She hadn't counted on spending another seven days with Ransom on this tiny island. She'd made it through one week, but she'd started out despising the man. Now she was wavering between admiration and downright affection. What an idiot she was! Ransom Shepard was a detached, untrusting, wealthy president of a corporation. They had nothing in common but a mutual imprisonment on a remote, befogged isle. She was a waitress with little education, and sadly lacking in the social graces required by a multimillionaire's wife.

Wife! She was aghast at how far some twisted part of her subconscious had gone with its fantasizing. Wife indeed! She spun away from her hazy view of the runway and began to head back in what she thought was the direction of the house. Another week! How could she survive it?

When she'd first met Ransom, she'd wanted to slice up the good-looking rogue and feed him to the fish. She wished she could conjure up a healthy loathing for him right now. She'd give anything for an unrelenting urge to spit in those devilish gray eyes. He might be aloof and skeptical of strangers, but once he kissed a woman, she stayed kissed—though for her own peace of mind she might prefer to return to the status of stranger.

And as for the kids, they were clean, well-behaved and doing chores without being asked. Still unable to believe it, she shook her head, and as she did, her damp curls brushed her cheeks. She ran a distracted hand through the wet riot of dark mahogany curls, blushing hotly with the memory of Ransom's teasing compliments about her hair.

She didn't know how many more of those light gallantries she could abide and still manage to evade the tempting trap of his allure. Last night during dinner, he'd been a charming companion. And the barbecued chicken had been heavenly. She'd spent an enjoyable evening laughing and talking naturally with him, and she'd found herself drawn even more strongly to the complicated, intelligent man.

Sara hoped desperately that he wouldn't turn that infernal smile on her this next week, or move toward her with that easy fluid stride, or glance at her with those sinful silver eyes.

She vowed she would resist his attraction with all her strength. Drat it! Nobody would dare suggest that Sara Eller didn't have strength of will. She'd raised Lynn single-handedly against tough odds, hadn't she? Surely remaining chaste for one measly week couldn't be a major problem.

A dark figure with a set of powerful shoulders appeared in the mist. Sara blanched as the shadowed form loomed before her. There was no mistaking Ransom—this towering phantom in the mist—prowling toward her with the grace of a jungle beast, though the fog prevented her from seeing his features. She shivered with unwanted excitement and took a protective step backward.

"Give up?" he queried softly.

Her eyes widened. *Give up what?* she mentally retorted, visions of her virginity being cast carelessly aside for one fiery interlude in his arms. "If you mean the plane," she stated weakly, "I suppose I must."

"What else would I mean?" he asked, drawing nearer.

She shuddered as their eyes locked. He was even more strikingly handsome than she recalled, his hair curling damply over his forehead. "W-why, n-nothing, nothing at all," she stammered.

His face seemed to inch closer, and Sara had the feeling he was going to kiss her. With a gasp, she stumbled a single step away, her body disobeying traitorously when she told herself to run. All she could manage to do was implore him with her eyes. They mustn't! *She* mustn't!

His kisses were too addictive, and she didn't dare allow herself a second taste. "No..." she whimpered, breathing in his scent as it mingled with the damp salty air. Unhappily she noted that her body had begun to tilt toward him against her will.

"No?" He inquired. "I would have thought you'd welcome this parka. Your jacket isn't warm enough for our weather."

She blinked in surprise, perceiving belatedly that he had been about to place the coat around her shoulders. Avoiding the possibility of his touch, she took the coat and slipped it on. "Thank you," she whispered, plunging her shaking hands into the pockets.

One corner of his mouth twisted up. "And I thought we'd gotten along so well last night."

He was right in his mild censure, of course. She was acting like a foolish schoolgirl. They *had* gotten along well last night. This immature craziness would have to stop.

"We did," she assured him, regaining her poise. "It's just my job—I'm worried about losing it," she fibbed.

"I'm sorry the phones are out, Sara. And I'm sorry Dorf didn't send the plane back for you," he offered close to her ear. "Sorrier than you know."

His melancholy tone was real. For once, there was no guile or teasing in his remark. Odd, but she had the feeling he was every bit as unhappy about the fog and Krukoff's absence as she.

He took her elbow to steer her away from the airstrip, and she chanced a furtive glance sideways at him. It startled her to see that he was quietly considering her with a brooding expression.

CHAPTER SEVEN

"WOULD YOU LIKE to walk on the beach?" Ransom asked as they headed toward the house.

A tremor of nervous anticipation shot down her spine. The last thing in the world she wanted was to take a walk with this man. She wanted—no, needed—to get away, far away. But she knew that asking again whether Krukoff might make the trip once the fog lifted would only lead to another of Ransom's caustic comments. She might as well face the fact that she was stuck on St. Catherine for another week. With a sigh that made no mystery of the fact that a stroll with Ransom was not at the top of her wish list, she murmured, "We might walk right into the ocean and drown."

His chuckle was strangely warm within the chilly cocoon of the fog. "Your enthusiasm is inspirational, Sara." Changing direction slightly and pulling her along with him, he added, "We'll be able to see well enough. Trust me."

She shifted her gaze ahead. There were no trees or buildings to use as landmarks—only the undulating tundra grasses and flowers, and a low bush here and there. It was true, though. She could see well enough not to drop off into oblivion without a yard or two of warning. "I thought you wanted me to stay the hell away from you." She bit her tongue. That little comment had come out of nowhere and had nothing to do with walking in fog. She swallowed, pulling her hand from his arm, praying he would let it pass without a tormenting remark.

He laughed curtly. She should have known; this man could never let anything that would serve to humble and distress her pass. "Ah," he murmured, "you remembered. My words come back to haunt me."

Surprising her, he retrieved her hand and replaced it along the inside of his elbow, curling her fingers over his arm before he let them go. "You'd better hold on. The way down to the beach is rocky."

She didn't pull away again, but endured his contact. Even the touch of his sweater mattered more to her than she dared acknowledge. Working for a verbal rift that would distance them emotionally, she charged, "Most women would recall a remark like that, don't you think?"

"You mean especially coming on the heels of my crude pass?" he asked, his tone more questioning than mocking.

She looked at him, trying to gauge his disposition. Was he teasing her again, or was he actually curious about her opinion? "Yes, *especially* coming on the heels of your crude pass," she repeated tightly.

"Was it that crude?" he inquired.

She couldn't tell by the sound of his voice if he was mocking her now or not, but she was sure he must be. Irked that he seemed to find so much pleasure in embarrassing her, she said, "I would think a man of your experience and education would be able to tell the difference between crude and gentlemanly behavior."

He came to an abrupt halt, forcing Sara to stop, too. When he peered down at her, his eyes were narrowed, his mouth hard. "You would think a man of my experience and education would know a lot of things, wouldn't you?" He grinned then, but though the show of teeth and his chiseled good looks were always a striking sight, the expression on his face was ominous. "Yes, you would think that," he said before beginning his trek again, dragging her with him.

Sara was confused. It was strange, but it seemed he wasn't reacting to her reproach as much as reproaching himself in some way. "What are we talking about?" she asked, bewildered, as they strode through the encompassing mist.

They reached the cliff. Ignoring her frustrated outburst, he instructed, "Take my hand and follow close behind me."

He headed down the steep rocky path as Sara clutched his fingers. She put aside her irritation in favor of trying not to fall to her death. In reality, it would be impossible for her to tumble the fifty feet without slamming into Ransom first. This stalwart man, clad in snug jeans, a white turtleneck sweater and hiking boots, would not be easy to budge, no matter how ungainly her descent. He seemed at home picking his way along the craggy path that led to the beach.

"I'll have to let you go for a minute," he said. "Hold on to that outcropping until I find better footing."

She did as he instructed and watched him scramble down about three feet to a ledge. When he was settled, he surprised her by reaching up and grasping her waist. "You'd better let go now. This wasn't meant to be a game of tug-of-war," he said, reminding her that she had a death grip on the jutting rock. Feeling stupid, she let go. Her only excuse was that she was so startled by the electric current that flared through her at the intimate contact of his hands on her waist, she'd frozen.

She was suspended in his arms for barely a second before he deposited her on the ledge beside him, but it seemed like a much longer, more significant span of time. They had been very near for a wink of eternity, their lips hovering, their eyes clinging—and then it had ended, but for the lingering touch of his hands. His fingers slid over the swell of her hips, tarrying there an instant too long to be an accident. She exhaled and shivered, her eyes going wide and struggling to focus in the general area of his broad chest.

When he finally released her, he asked, "Are you all right?"

She jumped. "I... Sure. Let's go on."

He took her hand with gentle authority, and this time she found herself savoring the feel of his fingers more than she'd ever savored a touch in her life. By merely lifting her down from a rock, Ransom had affected her totally—more than any other man's calculated attempts at seduction. Her body hummed in response, her lips tingled, as though she'd just been soundly kissed. What had his eyes said, his hands done, to make her yearn to be beneath him on the ground, his mouth pressed lovingly to hers?

She followed clumsily behind him now, her legs functioning like melting putty. She saw nothing on the way but his profile and the powerful sway of his shoulders as he descended with her in tow. She prayed she wouldn't embarrass herself and stumble against him like a lumbering cow. But she also prayed she *would* stumble against him. Though she was more behind than beside him, her mind orchestrated the fantasy so that he would instinctively turn as she fell and she would plunge into the solid heat of his chest, the encompassing protectiveness of his arms. She wanted to feel his fingers splayed across her back, moving, igniting, exploring secret, soft places she'd allowed no other man to—

"What?" she gasped, her voice a half whisper, half cry when she felt a burning touch on her cheek.

"I said, we're on the beach, you can let go of my hand," Ransom repeated, his expression curious. "Where did you go, Sara? Are you sure you're all right?"

The hand on her cheek slid away, leaving its impact in a scorching path along her mist-dampened jaw. His flesh always felt so enticingly warm against hers, like a steaming mug of hot chocolate pressed between cold hands after a dash through a Kansas blizzard. "I... Of course I'm all right. It's just that in Andover, we don't get much experience climbing mountains. I guess...I was concentrating on not falling," she lied, hoping it sounded plausible.

"I see," he said, his tone dubious. "Then you can quit concentrating now." A squeeze on her fingers told her she was still clutching his hand.

She released her hold as though his fingers had become a nest of wasps.

The ocean lapping against the beach and the faint calling of unseen seabirds filled the disconcerting gap of time while Sara picked invisible lint from the oversize parka she was wearing. She cleared her throat more than once, at a loss for anything casual and not incriminating to say. In desperation she headed toward the sea until she could see the foamy waves as they tumbled up the sand and then fell away, disappearing back into the fog. She stuffed her offending hand into her coat pocket. How awkward this was turning out to be. Why didn't she just wear a flashing neon sign that read I'm Infatuated With Ransom Shepard? It couldn't be any more blatant than her recent dull-witted behavior.

"So," Ransom asked, breaking through the quiet, "which way do you want to walk?"

She scanned the gray-shrouded world around her and shrugged. "What difference does it make?" She wasn't in the mood to care about such trivialities as directions.

"Good attitude," he agreed, sounding very near. "I have a feeling you would have had an opinion on the subject last week."

Curiosity getting the better of her, she twisted to face him. "Is that an insult?"

He lifted a shoulder casually. "In a way." Taking her arm and gently propelling her along the beach, he said, "We both suffer from the same malady, Sara."

She squinted at him, suspicious. "Oh? And what might that be?"

"We're both love—"

"Don't you dare suggest I'm love-starved," she protested, yanking her arm from his hold.

He glanced at her quizzically.

She backed away, chiding, "Who's coming on to whom this time?"

He moved to confront her directly, his gaze narrowing. "I was about to say we are both lovers of achievement. Workaholics. I had no intention of suggesting you were lovestarved. How would I know a thing like that?"

His stern candidness made her cringe, and she wished she could shrivel up and blow away, never to be seen again. How *would* he know such a thing? Of course he wouldn't. She'd given him superhuman powers to read minds, it appeared. Sick about revealing a glimpse of her lonely workaday life, she averted her gaze. When that didn't put enough distance between her and Ransom's looming presence, she began to trudge away from him.

"Sara," he called softly.

Taking his sympathetic tone as a show of pity, she spun around pointing accusingly at him. "And another thing. I said that about love-starved, not because I am love-starved, but because *you* are!" She knew she was spouting off about things better left unsaid, but she didn't want him to think for one moment that she was not a completely fulfilled woman of the nineties—no matter how flagrant a lie that might be. "You said it yourself. You need a woman. I should have steered clear of you. I'm no babe in the woods, I know that... that men are ruled by their hormones. I know—"

"Just what do you know, Sara?" he growled as long, familiar fingers grasped her wrist. Sara's eyes flew open. Until she'd felt Ransom's touch at her wrist and heard his menacing question, she hadn't realized she'd squeezed her eyes shut to staunch threatening tears.

"Tell me what you know," he repeated gruffly. "How love-starved am I? Am I so sexually frustrated that I'm likely to throw you on your back and ravage you on this beach? Is that what you think?"

She grew rigid, apprehension slicing through her as he took an intimidating step forward. She stared up at him, at hard eyes that gleamed like glacial ice, and she knew for the first time how really powerful a man he was and how helpless she was in the face of his rage. Self-defense class or no, it would be an impossible task to stop this man if he set his mind to having his way with her.

She blinked, her eyes large and liquid. "I...I..." she said brokenly. "You're hurting me, Ransom...."

That wasn't strictly true. In fact, he was holding her wrist tenderly. Still, he was so angry she anticipated pain and was positive that at any second he'd begin to squeeze.

"You don't know the meaning of suffering, darling," he whispered, rancor heavy in his tone. With a growled curse, he curled her arm behind her back, arching her against his body. Sara experienced a strange, sweet torture at the contact. His scent filled her brain, fogging her mind. "Dammit, Sara," he warned, his voice rumbling with restrained anger. "I'm doing my best to ignore the winsome innocence you flaunt—"

"Flaunt?" She echoed the odd word unaware she'd even spoken.

"I admit it. You're good. Better than any woman I've run up against in the past five years." He flashed a brief, contemptuous show of teeth.

Because she was unable to form a coherent thought, Sara said nothing.

"Dorf was right. I need the solace of a woman's body," he admitted roughly. "I haven't had a relationship with a woman since my wife's death." He paused, and Sara could feel the tension rampaging through him, the thudding of his heart. "The trouble is, I don't want another woman in my life. Except for those who'll offer me a little warmth in bed. Since you, knowing better, came on this walk with me, I thought you might have changed your mind. Have you decided to give me that warmth and ask for nothing in return but your own sexual satisfaction?" He lowered his head a fraction, his lips parting in mute invitation. "Can you say yes, Sara?" he asked.

She moistened dry lips, her gaze fixed on his wonderful mouth as it came nearer, ever nearer, with the languor of the passage of the sun across the sky. Her heart was hammering against her rib cage, and she knew he must be aware of her desire to touch that mouth again. But fear loomed, too. If she did, she knew she would be forever lost.

"Well?" he urged, his voice beguiling, his lazy, sexy smile sending her senses spinning. "Say yes," he coaxed, his heated breath tantalizing her cool lips.

She sighed as some woman somewhere replied with the most breathy yes she'd ever heard. It took a moment for Sara to recognize her own voice, and it horrified her to find the answer had come from her own uncontrollable lips. Appalled, she stammered, "I—I mean *no!*"

"I know what you mean," he assured her, a sudden frost hanging on the edge of his words. "And since I'm so damned love-starved, I may take you up on your offer." Nostrils flaring, he growled, "It's amazing what a fog can reveal, isn't it, Sara... my love." The sarcasm in his endearment was so sharp it made her flinch.

"One more thing," he said, his tone deceptively detached. "So you won't brand me less than a gentleman, keep to your right along the beach. The house isn't far."

She stumbled backward as she was abruptly released from his tenacious hold on her body and her soul. When she'd regained her balance, she cast her gaze around, bereft and forlorn. Ransom was nowhere to be seen.

Confused and too feeble to stand, she sank to the sand and cradled her head in her hands, trying to decipher what had just happened. "What did he mean, he knew what I meant?" she whispered brokenly. "I don't even know what I meant."

THE NEXT DAY dawned rainy but free of fog. Sara escaped the house unscathed. At least she didn't have an embarrassing run-in with Ransom. No doubt he was out making his rounds of the bird cliffs. "Just as well," she muttered raggedly.

Last night had been difficult, and dinner had been a stiff affair. Affair! The word conjured up heated visions of Ransom—his muscular body, that irresistible dimple in his chin, those silvery eyes—drawing her willingly into his arms murmuring soft endearments of undying love. Squelching the thought, she yanked up the hood of her parka. Undying love, indeed! The man was completely self-centered as far as lovemaking was concerned. And if his ego had been a volcano, its eruption would blot out the sun forever!

Ohh! She simply couldn't stand him. Pain or no pain, grief or no grief, a person could only take so much indignity. And Sara had taken her share and more from Ransom Shepard. That little scene on the beach had been unforgivable. *He'll take me up on my offer!* She sniffed derisively. *The jerk should live so long!*

By his black scowl and clipped conversation at dinner, even Lynn and Tag were beginning to sense fierce tension between them. The evening meal had been uncomfortably rigid. And Sara decided that was just fine with her. The less conversation she had with the bothersome Mr. Shepard during this final week of captivity, the better.

Hearing youthful laughter, she headed down to the beach where Lynn and Tag were cavorting with Baby and Boo. As she was about to make herself known, Tag took off his ball cap and tossed it into the sea.

Sara stared, perplexed. "What did you do that for?"

He pointed toward the dark water. "Watch."

She squinted, losing sight of the cap as it floated on the indulating surface. "What am I watching?" she asked, moving up beside him.

Without warning, something lunged from the depths, lifting the cap skyward. Just as quickly, both the beast and Tag's ball cap disappeared, only to resurface time and again on the snout of some large fish. It was heading down the beach, but staying some fifty feet out.

"What's going on?" Sara asked.

"Come on!" shouted Lynn as she sprinted along the sand in the same direction as the sea creature.

Sara shook her head, but began to jog after the two teens. A few minutes later, when she rounded a bend, she saw Tag picking his way along a peninsula. At the very end of the rocky outcropping, he stood tall, held out his hand and called, "Potluck!"

Surging up from the water came the beast, depositing the soggy cap in Tag's outstretched fingers.

Lynn shrieked with glee, clapping her hands. "What a smart dolphin." She turned to Sara and exclaimed. "He taught Tag that trick."

Sara watched the boy make his way back to the beach. "Who taught Tag that trick?"

"Potluck! He's a dolphin," Lynn said. "Tell her Tag."

He shook saltwater from his cap before clapping it back on his head. "The first day Dad and I got here, the wind blew my cap off. I saw this dolphin catch it and head off with it. Since it was my favorite cap, I followed and yelled at him to bring it back." He smiled sheepishly. "'Course I didn't expect to ever see the cap again, but I got down here to Sea Lion Cove and he was swimming around." Pointing toward the arm of rock, he said, "So, I went out there and yelled at him to bring me back my hat. And darned if he didn't!"

"See?" Lynn giggled. "Tag learned a trick."

He punched her playfully in the arm. "Oh, yeah? I see you ain't learned nothin' yet."

She punched back. "I learned not to get my hat wet."

"It's been raining all morning. Your hat's wet, too, dummy."

"Dummy!" Lynn chirped. "Who washed his red shirt with his white underwear, Mr. Pink Panties?"

Tag lunged at Lynn, and she squealed, taking off down the beach.

"I'll get you for that, Motormouth!"

Sara found herself abandoned, as Tag, Lynn, Boo and Baby scampered off. She sighed, unable to shake a heavy feeling of forlornness that had shrouded her ever since her fight with Ransom. One bright spot, she noticed, was that the rain had stopped and there was a break in the clouds. A shaft of sunshine made the sand sparkle like broken bits of smoked glass. The air around her held the scent of salt, lush plantlife and the faintest hint of warmth. Except for the fact that she would have to wile away the hours in the same time zone as Ransom, this might turn out to be a pretty day.

"Hey, you down there!" shouted a woman from the direction of Ransom's house.

Sara looked up to see someone with long dark hair waving at her, "Up here," the woman called again. "I came to visit."

She smiled encouragingly, so Sara hurried up the easy incline from the beach and came face-to-face with a lovely young woman. She had a round face, black eyes and straight black hair, thickly plaited into a single braid that hung over her shoulder almost to her waist. There was a child, a boy of about two, sitting on the thick mat of lush tundra vegetation beside a big basket and a metal cooking pot. When the child saw Sara, he picked up the empty basket and held it out to her, laughing.

"Hello," the woman said, offering a welcoming hand. "I'm Lilly Merculieff. I know we'll meet in a couple of days at the Halibut Festival, but I couldn't wait." She indicated the direction of the village. "I'm from town, in case you haven't guessed. Since Rance went fishing with my husband, Dan, I thought you might like some company. How'd you like to gather eggs and berries with me?'' She shrugged and grinned. ''It's sort of a woman's thing around here—if we want to eat, that is. The guys brag and fish. We women gossip and gather.''

Sara smiled, happy for anything to take her mind off Ransom. ''I'd love to help,'' she said. ''But what's the Halibut Festival?''

''Oh, hasn't Rance mentioned it?'' Hoisting her son, who still clutched the empty basket, she said, ''He will. It's this weekend. We celebrate the beginning of summer. Everybody comes.'' She indicated the pot. ''Mind carrying that? Danny's getting pretty heavy.''

''I don't mind,'' Sara said, scooping up the big pot. A rush of excitement skittered through her at the idea of going to an island party. She only hoped Ransom intended to invite her and her sister. As things stood now, she wasn't all that sure. ''What's this for?'' she asked, gesturing at the pot.

''Mossberries. I'll show you after we get the eggs.''

They headed back toward town along the cliffs. Danny, chunky and dark-eyed with wispy hair standing up all over his head, was alternately carried or, when he get too cranky, allowed to scamper along with the two women as they hiked. The walk was pleasant, and as they went, the cliffs grew treacherous before petering out to a mild rocky slope.

''I've wanted to meet you,'' Lilly said. ''I saw Lynn in town a couple of times. She's a little handful, isn't she?''

Sara laughed. ''A big handful, actually.''

''Oh!'' Lilly exclaimed, pointing. ''There're our guys. In the red outboard.'' She waved and shouted.

Both men looked up and waved back. Sara didn't know quite what to do, so she lifted an arm in mute response. ''I thought your fishing boats were bigger than that,'' she remarked more to herself than to Lilly.

"They are. That's Dan's outboard, strictly for fishing on a quiet afternoon with a buddy."

Sara pulled her eyes from Ransom. Even far out on the placid surface of the Bering Sea, he was a formidable-looking man.

"It's good to see Dan and Rance together again," Lilly went on, "Dan was Rance's best friend when the Shepards visited every summer. It's been too long since he's been to his family's place."

There was a pensive sigh on Lilly's voice, and Sara had to ask, "I understand his wife's death was hard on him."

Lilly nodded solemnly. "Yes. They were so happy. I've never seen a man take to married life as well as Rance did. He adored Jill so."

Jill? So that had been his wife's name.

Lilly frowned as though she'd spoken out of turn. Touching Sara's arm, she said, "Listen, I'm sorry. But naturally you know about the accident."

Sara nodded, and Lilly brightened. "Anyway, we're all glad he's finally coming out of his depression over Jill's death and, well, with you here and all..."

Sara blinked, not understanding.

"I mean when we heard you'd come out here to spend some time with him, we were happy he'd found someone, that's all." She pointed to a spot near the cliff. "Over there's a good spot for gathering eggs. I'll go down and hand them up to you. Okay? Then we'll split 'em later. Half for you and half for me." She turned to her toddler. "Danny, sugar, you sit here and wait for mama." She fished a lollipop from her coat pocket and handed it to him.

The boy plopped down obediently and began to tear at the cellophane wrapper. Sara wordlessly followed Lilly's lead, but when they got to the cliff and the black-haired woman began descending, she said, "I think there's been some misunderstanding, Lilly. I didn't come here to visit Ransom. I'd never even met him until I got to the island. My sister ran away from home and came up here in answer to an ad for a mail-order bride. Tag's idea. And since the phones are out and the fog kept Krukoff from flying in yesterday, we're stuck."

Lilly looked up. "You're kidding!" Her dark eyes grew wide. "Tag advertised for a new mother?" She scanned Sara, then smiled again, this time with sympathy. "Poor kid. I never could figure out why Rance sent him away to that school. You'd think, when someone you love dies, you'd cling to your kid." She glanced lovingly at her son. "I know I would. Any mother would."

Sara nodded, frowning. "There's something wrong between them. But I can't figure out what it is."

"Yeah," Lilly agreed sadly. "When Dan asked if he wanted Tag to go fishing with them, Rance got this hard look on his face and said no." She reached into a nest and took out two long eggs, white with gray spots, leaving one. "I can't figure it out." She sighed, handing the eggs up to Sara. "Men aren't like women. When we're sad, we surround ourselves with friends and family, bond, cry and heal, while men run off and lick their wounds alone, all the time insisting they're just fine—some stupid macho thing, I guess."

Sara carefully placed the eggs in the basket. "I guess," she echoed, not convinced it was as simple as that—though it was clear Ransom was still grieving over his wife's death. *He adored Jill.* No wonder he was so aloof, so determined not to let another woman into his life. He'd been hurt too badly to chance being hurt again. She sighed, surprised at how melancholy the sound was.

Lilly passed her two more eggs, remarking, "You like him, don't you?"

Startled by the perceptive statement, Sara blushed. "I hardly know him," she returned too quickly.

Lilly smiled. "I wish you luck," she said kindly. "Rance is too great a guy to waste his life mourning."

Sara swallowed to ease a sudden lump in her throat, then quickly changed the subject. "What kind of eggs are these?"

"Sea gull, honey." She reached into another nest and came up with two eggs that were light green with black spots and handed them to Sara.

"These look spoiled," Sara said, making a face.

Lilly laughed. "They're murre eggs. They taste better than they look."

Sara saw another nest near Lilly, but noticed she was leaving the eggs alone. "Why don't you want those?" she asked, pointing.

"Oh, those are kittiwake eggs," Lilly said. "I could. They're not endangered—yet—but they're threatened. The kittiwake population's down because overfishing of pollock by foreign companies has reduced their food source. They do what's called bottom-dragging—"

Deep-pitched shouting drew their attention, and both women turned toward the calm sea. One of the men in the red boat was struggling, his rod curved downward into the water and whipping to and fro. "Ransom," Sara whispered aloud. "What's wrong, Lilly?" she asked, her voice taking on a fearful squeak.

"I'd say he's hooked a halibut." Handing Sara four more green-and-black eggs, she said, "Those babies can weigh up to three hundred pounds. But this one looks to be around eighty or ninety."

"Oh, my!" Sara exclaimed. "Is he in danger?"

Lilly turned to stare at Sara, then burst out laughing. "Yeah, if you mean the halibut."

"How big is a ninety-pound halibut?" Sara asked, hoping her anxiety over Ransom's safety hadn't been too obvious.

"Probably three, three and a half feet."

"What'll we do with it?" Sara mused aloud. "I've never even cleaned a trout."

"No problem. We island women smoke the catch, then dry and salt it. We all share. Like I said, we pretty much live off the land here. And sometimes pickings get pretty slim." She plucked another two sea gull eggs from a fresh nest and handed them to Sara, adding with a grin, "Except for the wonderful smoked salmon Rance gives everybody at Christmastime."

A speculative gleam came into Lilly's eyes as she suggested softly, "You may hardly know him, but you've got it bad, don't you?" It wasn't a question.

At a loss as to how to answer, Sara sat back on her heels and shrugged. "Like you said, Lilly, he's still grieving for his wife. I'd be pretty foolish to fall for him, wouldn't I?"

Hearing a loud "whoop!" and masculine laughter, they peered back out over the sparkling water toward the red outboard in time to see a huge fish being drawn into the boat. Dan was helping with some sort of lethal-looking hook on a stick.

Sara sighed, relieved. "What's that thing Dan's got?" she asked.

"A gaff. Fish was bigger than I thought," Lilly replied, squealing with delight and waving to the men. After a minute, when the fish was safely in the bottom of the boat, Lilly turned and grinned at Sara, but there was compassion in her intelligent black eyes. Clambering up over the cliff to the grass, she stood and wiped grime from her jeans. "You never know about the future, Sara. Maybe Rance'll figure out he'd be a fool to let you slip through his fingers. Personally I think he would be."

Taking the basket from Sara's grip and grabbing her son by his sticky little fingers, she said, "Okay, Danny, let's you and me and Miss Sara go pick some mossberries." She gave Sara an sympathetic look. "And maybe do a little female bonding..."

Embarrassed, Sara wanted to talk about something else. "Where are these berries?" she asked hurriedly.

"On moss," Lilly replied, pointing farther along the cliff. "There's a great patch over there."

"You have berries that grow on moss?" Sara was astonished.

"Uh-huh. They're little black berries that taste a lot like grapes. Make great jams and desserts."

Sara shook her head. Berries that grew on moss. "Wait till the folks back in Kansas hear about this."

Lilly laughed her hearty open laugh and offered, "I'll give you my favorite recipe for jam, if you'd like." She turned to catch Sara's eye. "Rance loves mossberry jam."

Sara smiled helplessly. "Thanks. I love to cook." What she didn't say was that she doubted that Ransom's grief over his wife could be wiped away by a jar of mossberry jam simply because it was made by a woman with an absurd infatuation for him.

Her misgivings must have shown on her face, for Lilly smiled good-naturedly. "You don't think jam'll do it, huh?" She shrugged. "Stranger things have happened, honey. So, I'm giving you the recipe, anyway. Half the berries we pick'll be yours, minus what Danny—the fruit freak—eats."

They heard a shout of triumph and peered back out to sea. Ransom was fighting another battle with some unknown entity of the deep.

"Wow!" Lilly cried. "The man attracts 'em like a magnet."

Sara moved her gaze away, wishing fish were *all* Ransom attracted....

CHAPTER EIGHT

LATE THE NEXT MORNING, Sara set off on a hike. She had no particular goal in mind and eventually found herself beside a tranquil lagoon midway between Ransom's house and the village, with its quaint buildings and strange half-buried onion-domed church. Ransom had gone before she'd awakened, and she had no idea where he'd disappeared to. No doubt he was avoiding her just as she'd been avoiding him.

A stiff breeze was blowing the wave foam back into the sea on her left. She glanced to the right in time to see a scruffy, blue-black arctic fox appear over a ridge about a hundred yards away. As it sniffed the air, another short-snouted fox appeared and also tested the air. She found it hard to swallow the mossberry she'd just plucked as a cold finger of dread touched her spine. Since she'd been on the island, she'd seen foxes scampering around as they'd scavenged for food. However, there had always been only one at a time. That had been hard enough for her to deal with. But two?

Arctic foxes weren't very big or ferocious-looking as wild beasts went, but Sara was all too aware that even small domestic dogs bit when provoked. She carried with her a childhood fear of dogs, having been bitten badly when she was only four by a dog who didn't appreciate having its tail pulled. The scars still remained—on her palm and in her mind.

Because of her father's coaxing, Sara had made friends with the dog, but somehow, she'd never mastered her fear of unfamiliar animals. And these foxes were wild—not to mention always hungry. Glancing down at herself, she wondered vaguely if a redhead in a man's navy parka looked appetizing to a pair of foxes. Gnawing on her lower lip, she couldn't decide if it would be better to sit still or to run for her life.

As she waited, statue stiff, another fox appeared, and then another. She pondered the sudden congregation. As she watched in growing fear, the four wild animals seemed to locate her at the same time, for all at once a quartet of dark snouts pointed in her direction. Her blood froze in her veins. She was sitting amid a fragrant patch of blue lupines, a few feet from the calm water of the lagoon. The slope behind her was very steep. She would have to scramble madly up the last few feet and probably die of a heart attack as the charging beasts took their first nips out of her backside.

Her lips parted with apprehension as yet another fox appeared over the crest of the hill. Five against one. Sara didn't know much about arctic foxes. She knew they were wild, and she knew they were always looking for food. She only hoped they knew that humans weren't *beneath* them on Mother Nature's food chain.

As the animals cautiously approached, she managed to struggle to her feet. Making a shooing motion, she squealed, "Go 'way. If it'll help, I'm a staunch advocate of faux fur..."

Two of the animals cocked their heads to one side. One humorless brute bared sharp teeth.

"Maybe you're right. Not a good subject," Sara babbled, taking a prudent step away. Intending to make a judicious yet swift exit, she slid on the damp surface and fell, her hip striking an exposed slab of volcanic rock. Stifling a moan, she watched in despair as her life flashed before her eyes.

Two of the largest, bravest foxes began to trot toward her, and she stared in terror, visualizing herself as brunch for this horde of blunt-bodied killers. She'd always thought that when a person was in imminent danger of being eaten by wild beasts, the time just prior to the event would pass in slow motion. Not so. Those greedy-eyed devils were upon her with the speed of teenagers on a free pizza. The first two lunged, and a scream was torn from her throat as she threw up her arms to protect her face.

She felt a strong tug at her parka and yelled again, trying to rise to her feet before their teeth cut through the nylon fabric and met her flesh.

In the next instant, she was lifted to a standing position by a strong grip on one elbow. When she blinked up to see Ransom standing there, she leapt on him in a last-ditch effort to survive. "Oh!" she cried in panic. "Run, Ransom! I'm being eaten alive!"

His arms went around her waist, but the added support was hardly necessary to keep her aloft. She'd thrown both her arms and legs about him in her attempt to clamber out of the reach of her attackers. The tugging on her parka continued, and she tightened her hold on her rescuer. "Run!" she implored him. "They'll get you, too!"

"I can't run in this position," he said quietly.

"Well, you can try!" she pleaded. "Our lives depend on it!"

"Hold on for a minute." His tone had become an odd mixture of concern and mirth. "I have to let go of you with one hand."

She buried her face in the hollow of his throat and did as he commanded, clutching for dear life.

Though her mind was on survival, she noticed vaguely that his hand slid along her side and into the pocket of the parka she was wearing. After a minute, the tugging at her coat ceased, and the foxes' guttural growls diminished.

"Sara," he murmured as his arm returned to hold her, "I think you'll live now."

"Did you shoot them with a silencer?" she asked, confused as to how he'd gotten rid of them with no overt violence.

"Shoot them? Why, they're adorable."

"Adorable?" At the memory of her near death she clutched him even tighter. "I suppose you'd think being strangled by a boa constrictor would be a laugh a minute."

His chuckle resonated through her rigid body. "Sara," he repeated. "Please unwrap your legs from around my hips."

"Are you sure the attack's over?" she asked weakly.

He cleared his throat. "As far as the foxes are concerned, yes." His voice was unusually husky. Still clinging with her arms, she slowly lowered her legs to the ground and peered around.

There were now seven foxes milling about at their feet, eating some undistinguishable substance. Befuddled with fright, she could only stare. After a few seconds, she felt her arms being removed from Ransom's shoulders, his strong fingers locking about her wrists. Suddenly recalling their feud, she jerked away.

He was grinning at her, and she flushed. "What's so funny? I was almost killed by hunger-crazed wild animals, and you think it's funny?"

He ran a fist across his mouth and the smile disappeared, though Sara knew he had to struggle to keep a straight face. "Well?" she demanded. "Do you hate me so much you think it's humorous when I'm practically devoured alive?"

He tilted his head in her direction. "That parka you're wearing. It's not the one I loaned you."

She looked at him in irritation. "What are you, the fashion police? No, it's not. The parka you gave me to wear is fluff-drying with a pair of sneakers. I got it muddy, so I borrowed this one out of the hall closet. Why?"

"Because that's one of my parkas, and the foxes recognized it."

"Oh? So they were trying to kill *you?* I can't say I'm surprised."

His gaze was now openly amused. "You do hold a grudge, don't you?" He shook his head at her. "I keep a sack of dried sea-lion meat in the pocket of that coat to feed to the foxes when they chance by. They were merely going for their treat, not your throat."

Treat? Dubious, she reached into the pocket and felt a sack. Inside it she fingered shards of leathery matter. So, what he said was true.

He cleared his throat. "Apparently, red-haired vixens are more excitable than blue-black ones. I've never been jumped before."

She frowned, perplexed. Jumped? None of the foxes had jumped... Then the whole dreadful episode rushed back with crystal clarity. Her gaze rocketed to meet his twinkling eyes, and her cheeks sizzled with mortification. The stark truth was that moments ago she'd actually *jumped* the man!

Taking a mental lunge toward self-preservation, she veered as far from what they were both thinking as she could manage, challenging, "How was I to know you keep meat in your coat pocket! Who keeps meat in their pockets?"

"I—"

"I know *you* do," she blustered, frustrated by his nonchalance. "I mean, why don't you wear the darned coat, then?"

"It was insensitive of me to leave it in the closet," he said, looking unrepentant. "I'm a thoughtless brute."

"You're incorrigible," she charged, and spun away. As she was about to stalk off, she noticed that one of the departing foxes was dragging a large cloth bundle through the grasses. "What's that?" she breathed, afraid of the answer.

"Bread," Ransom said.

Reluctantly she faced him. "Bread?"

He shrugged dismissively. "This morning was the monthly bake sale in the village. That was the bread I bought."

As she watched the bundle being dragged away toward some unseen den, she felt twinge of guilt. "You dropped it to rescue me?"

He nodded. "No problem. They'll have another sale next month. Of course, I won't be here...."

She detected his wistful tone and had to smile. So the man had a weakness. "Well, well, the salmon tycoon likes fresh bread," she teased, enjoying having the upper hand for once.

His half smile was boyishly charming. "Yes. Warm, fresh homemade bread."

"And now a month's supply is ruined."

"Fresh-baked goods do lose a little of their appeal when they're dragged through mud."

She eyed him thoughtfully. "I'll bake you some bread—and Lilly gave me her recipe for mossberry jam."

His expression grew curious—and, also, cautious. "Oh?" he asked. "And I suppose you have a price for this service?"

"I do." She came to stand right in front of him and gave him a disdainful I've-finally-got-you-where-I-want-you smile. "I'll bake you some bread and make a batch of jam, but you've got to quit teasing me."

"Me?" His smiling face was the picture of innocence.

"That's just the sort of remark I mean!"

He flashed his teeth, full of the devil. "I don't know, Sara. That's a lot to ask. There are so few diversions on the island."

She poked his chest for emphasis. "*And* you have to quit talking like we're going to have an affair," she blurted, then bit her tongue, wishing she hadn't gone quite that far. All this time, she hadn't been able to forget those disturbing moments on the beach when he'd taken her into his arms and goaded her into saying things she didn't mean—at least, things she hoped she didn't mean. With trepidation, she forced her gaze to remain locked on his.

"Well?" she demanded, her bravado as weak as her voice.

He said nothing for a long while, his eyes watchful, unreadable. Braving it out, she glared at him, nervous to the point of light-headedness but refusing to be the first to look away.

Without warning, he dragged her into his arms, claiming her lips as he crushed her to his chest. His kiss was hard yet gentle, triumphant yet searching, and it sent delightful sensations spiraling through her. Even in her exasperation, she was shocked by her wild response. Her body sang with the joy of renewal, and she was struck by the awful reality that she'd been desperate for this to happen again.

She moaned against his mouth. Just as she gave herself fully to him, circling his neck with her arms, opening her lips in invitation, he jerked away from her, leaving her lips burning with an unquenchable fire. Her emotions whirled and careered, her mind clouding with confusion and need.

"Just for the record, Sara," he muttered, his tone tainted with husky desire. "I don't bribe easily."

She blinked, trying to make heads or tails of a spinning world. By the time she could see straight, he was walking away from her, his movements swift and powerful. For a long time, she could only stare stupidly after him. But when full realization hit, she sagged, groaning. What was with him? He baited her, then withdrew, teased and tempted, then stalked off. Numbed to her core, Sara watched him disappear over the rise. It was depressingly clear that Ransom's sexual needs were warring against his loyalty to his wife's memory; unfortunately for Sara, her heart was being trampled to bits on the battlefield.

"HALIBUT FESTIVAL?" shouted Tag. "Today?" He scooted up to his father who was spooning rice into a pan lined with piecrust. "You're not kidding, are you, Dad?"

Tag's outburst halted Sara on her way through the living room and, curious she moved back to the kitchen doorway to watch as Ransom said, "I thought I mentioned it."

"Heck, no." Tag yelped with delight. "Hey, Lynn. Halibut Festival!"

"I heard you," Lynn said, shoving breakfast dishes into an overhead cabinet. "Good grief, people in Africa heard you. Quit yelling."

Tag snickered. "But it's a great party. Lots of food, games and rad music."

Sara leaned against the doorjamb as Tag handed Lynn a dish he'd just dried and said, "And dad's making fish pie."

Lynn moved over to the table to inspect what Ransom was doing. "Smells like it," she groused.

"I know, it stinks right now," Tag admitted. "But when it's cooked it's great."

"Thanks for the vote of confidence, Taggart," Ransom said as he began to place pieces of raw halibut on top of the cooked rice. "But it's been years since I've made my mother's recipe. Might taste like old gym socks."

Tag took hold of Lynn's sleeve. "Five of the high school guys have a band called Hot Scum. They sound like that awesome heavy-metal-punk group Putrid Galoshes."

"Totally radical!" Lynn gushed.

"Don't forget some of *my* high school friends will play later on," Ransom added as he sprinkled onions over the fish. "They can play anything from big-band to Eric Clapton to Buddy Holly and the Crickets."

"Crickets? What a gross name for a band," Lynn complained, her face screwed up in distaste.

Ransom's laughter was rich and full-bodied, and Sara felt a twinge of hurt. He hadn't even smiled at her since yesterday, when he'd so soundly kissed her after "rescuing" her from the foxes. She supposed he had no intention of inviting her to the festival. Apparently his loyalty to his wife's memory had been the victor in his emotional battle, and as far as he was concerned, she could stay home and play three-handed bridge with Baby and Boo.

Stuffing her hands into her pockets, she went to her bedroom to gather up her laundry. Lynn and Tag had done their loads earlier that morning, freeing the washer and dryer only moments ago.

As she stood in the tiny laundry room sorting her colored things from her whites, she sensed a presence at her back. Rubbing the nape of her neck, she twisted around to find Ransom standing there. He wasn't quite frowning, but didn't appear to be the happiest of men, either.

"Hello," he murmured.

She nodded stiffly. As though some demon deep inside wanted her to humiliate herself, she became fumble-fingered and dropped a camisole. Both she and Ransom watched as the pink froth of underwear fluttered down and came to rest on top of his hiking boots.

Mortified, she swooped to retrieve it, but as she took hold of a strap, so did he, and their hands brushed. When she recovered her balance, she noticed unhappily that the camisole was dangling from his long bronze fingers. His expression was watchful but unreadable. So what, Sara lamented inwardly. Why should things be any different this time? He was probably having a private little laugh-fest.

With self-conscious dispatch, she snatched her underwear from his hand and stuffed it into the washer.

"Sara," he murmured.

"What?" she inquired more snappishly than she would have liked, since she didn't want him to guess how strongly his touch affected her.

"About this afternoon."

She busied herself measuring detergent. "If you're referring to the festival, I heard. Go. Have a good time. Don't worry about me."

There was a long pause. Sara filled it by tossing more things into the washer—white, red, black, green. She didn't care. All she wanted was to have Ransom leave so that she could think clearly again.

"I'm taking a fish pie," he said quietly.

"I hope you two will be very happy," she mumbled, bending over the washer and absently arranging clothes.

"When I do a load of laundry, I just dump everything in and turn it on," he said, sounding very near. "You work harder at arranging clothes in the washing machine than anyone I've ever known."

Isn't it obvious I don't want to look at you? her mind shrieked. *If I have to stay here all day slumped over this darned machine, I will. Go away!* But all she said was, "If you have something to do somewhere far, far away, don't let me keep you."

He said nothing, but the nape of her neck continued to prickle with awareness of him. Finally, unable to withstand the stress his quiet closeness caused her, she spun to face him and demanded, "What are you trying to do? Drive me crazy? If you want to say something, spit it out! If you just want to hang around the laundry room, I'll be out of your way in a minute."

He was a compelling presence, yet there was an air of isolation about him, as though he'd built himself an electrified fence to stand behind. You could see him, but you could not touch him—not if you valued your sanity.

His faint smile held a trace of sadness. "I'm not interested in loitering in the laundry room. I wanted to know if you'd bake some bread for the festival. It's kind of potluck. Everyone on the island brings something." He added solemnly, "You needn't spend any time with me. There'll be a lot of young men there who would enjoy your company."

For an instant an odd yearning seemed to steal into his expression. Or had it? She searched his face, but saw nothing of the desire she'd thought she'd seen. Had it been mere wishful thinking?

"Sara?" he asked softly.

"Uh, of course, I'll make some bread. I'll make my hearty whole-grain bread," she stated briskly. "When should it be ready?"

"The festival starts at one. The beach isn't far. We'll walk." He paused, his lips quirking wryly. "I've tasted those hearty whole-grain breads. They tend to be pretty heavy. Are we going to need a forklift to carry yours?"

She was surprised that he'd made an effort to lighten the mood and eyed him narrowly. Though she refused to smile, her glower became less hostile. She didn't know how Ransom did it, but somehow he'd managed to break the tension between them with his small joke. Shaking her head, she protested, "That's the puniest attempt at humor I've ever heard."

Mild amusement flickered in his eyes. "Careful Sara. Such honeyed words might turn my head."

Rolling her eyes, she groaned, "Egomaniac. A kick in the shins would probably turn your head."

His expression darkened. As he moved to go, he said, "I'm a man, Sara, not a masochist."

AT ONE O'CLOCK, Sara removed her bread, steamy and smelling delicious, from the oven. A few minutes later, her contribution to the festival wrapped and put in a basket, she joined the others at the front door.

Ransom was holding his fish pie in one hand and the doorknob with the other. As soon as Lynn and Tag were outside, they ran on ahead. The weather had become overcast and foggy, a perfect complement to Sara's mood. Engulfed in an uncomfortable silence, Ransom and Sara hiked side by side toward the beach. After ten minutes, something flickered in the murky distance.

"I see them," Ransom said.

"Me, too," Sara replied, knowing he was referring to the soft distant glow of three bonfires on the dark sand. Keeping her eyes straight ahead, she asked, "What do you burn, considering there are not trees on the island?"

"Driftwood, discarded packing crates. Any wood scraps." There was a break in his explanation when Sara could hear only the whispering sound of their footsteps as they trod through the thick grasses. "It's said," he began again, "that one can find a beautiful woman behind every tree on St. Catherine Island. And every man in the village will be quick to say he cut down the last tree looking for one."

She squinted in puzzlement, hoping the fog would mask her curiosity, but it didn't. "It's a local joke," he explained.

"Why didn't you tell me the joke, then, and say *you* cut down the last tree? It wasn't funny the way you said it."

He shrugged. "Maybe because I'm not in the market for beautiful women."

She stumbled slightly, upset and not sure why. What had she wanted? Some sort of mindless flattery? Maybe she'd wanted him to ask, *Why should I look for a beautiful woman behind a tree when you're here, my lovely Sara?* Had she lost her mind? The man wasn't interested in her, not really. Maybe he thought she was worthy of warming his bed briefly, but certainly not worthy of much effort. Unable to stop herself, she asked, "Why bring it up at all, then?"

"What?"

"The beautiful women thing. Why bring it up?"

"Why not? It's a local joke."

She shrugged and looked away.

"What would you have me say?" he queried. "You know you're beautiful. Do you need to hear men tell you?"

She tightened her fingers around the basket handle and kept her eyes glued to the undulating landscape ahead of them. Did he really think she was beautiful?

"We fish for halibut on this island, Sara, not compliments."

"I—I've never fished for a compliment in my life," she defended herself, upset that he thought she'd wanted such a thing, although every word he'd said was true. Even in her distress, a glow of satisfaction warmed the pit of her stomach. Ransom Shepard had said she was beautiful. She wanted to curl up and die with contentment, to soar in the sky, to sob and laugh, but all she did was swallow several times and rasp, "If you'll recall, I didn't bring up the subject."

"Anybody who asks about where we get our wood gets that joke. It's a knee-jerk reaction."

She raised diffident eyes for an instant to discover that he was watching her. Dropping her glance, she retorted, "I'm sorry I asked."

The rest of the trek to the beach was shrouded with oppressive quiet. As they approached, the noise of the festive villagers grew louder, only serving to magnify Sara's downcast mood.

When they neared the first roaring bonfire, she plastered on a grin and pretending to be as cheerful as the dark-haired, dark-eyed Aleuts Ransom was introducing her to. He, too, had adopted a laughing and bantering demeanor, but Sara could detect the truth. His dusky eyes smoldered with discontent.

The afternoon passed quickly, with a sack race, three-legged race, tug-of-war, volleyball tournament and enough food to keep a rocketship full of astronauts fat and sassy on a trip to Pluto.

By nine o'clock, Sara was so full she felt like a beached whale. She'd sampled everything from raw halibut eaten with native wild celery called *pooch-key,* to numerous kinds of roasted, boiled, barbecued and dried island meats. One of her favorite discoveries was a deep-fried bread called *aladekes* and another local jam made from cloudberries. She sighed heavily, wishing she'd enjoyed the food a bit less. But after all, it was a festival, and Sara had to admit she couldn't remember when she'd had such a good time.

She lounged in her folding chair amid other adults who were watching from the sidelines as their teenagers, home for the summer from school in Anchorage, danced to the raucous disharmony of Hot Scum. The teens seemed to thrive on the whiny discord, twitching and lunging as though they were having an allergic reaction to the very air. Sara was hard put not to hold her ears as the five animated members of Hot Scum slithered and jumped, grimaced and screeched out their rendition of "Yin-yang Mama."

"What do you suppose that means?" shouted Lilly Merculieff, her toddler wriggling in her lap.

Sara shook her head. "I think it's best we don't know."

Both women laughed and relaxed as the teenagers cavorted on the sand. Sara was amazed to see her chubby sister flailing about as if her freckled body had been possessed by a gawky fertility goddess. The spectacle wasn't up to even the most gullible's standards for erotica, but it was... interesting. Sara wondered if, as a teen, she, too, had exhibited that same ungainly pseudo-sexy picture when she'd boogied to pop music. The thought made her burst out laughing.

"What's so funny?"

She looked up to see Ransom standing beside her chair. Wiping away her smile, she shrugged. "Nothing. Just watching the kids slough off a million years of evolution."

Her last shouted word came out a trifle loud, for Hot Scum had reached the clamoring end of their abuse of the human eardrum.

"Whew!" Lilly exclaimed with relief. "Now Dan's band takes over, and we old folks can have some fun." She scooped up her son and gave Ransom a bright smile. "Nice to have you back at one of these, Rance." Glancing at Sara with not-very-subtle approval, she said, "Enjoy the dance."

Ransom smiled at her and took the seat she'd vacated. "Enjoying yourself?" he asked as Hot Scum left the platform and an older group of shaggy-haired musicians took their place.

Sara nodded. "Nice people, your Pribilovians."

"They seem to like you, too."

Wondering at the slight edge to his voice, she pretended to take special note of the thirty-something drummer as he sat down and set up his equipment. Had Ransom been bothered by the fact that several of the island bachelors had monopolized Sara that afternoon? Had it troubled him that she'd won the three-legged race partnered with a very nice young man named George? Probably not, considering he'd had no problem finding attentive female companionship. Still, his tone had been, well, peculiar. Unsure of what to say, she murmured, "Food's good."

"Pretty soon they're going to start grilling halibut for dinner," Ransom said.

She couldn't avoid looking at him anymore. "Dinner?" she repeated in an agonized whisper. "More food?"

He appeared casually amused. "We're celebrating the beginning of summer, and looking forward to a good halibut season. The festival will go on until early in the morning."

Her mouth fell open, but she had no response.

He smiled. "When we Pribilovians party, we party."

"Apparently." She allowed herself a long, weary sigh.

Music began to drift from the bandstand. Sara concentrated on trying to recognize the tune, but failed. When the audience started to sing along, she realized they were doing so in a language unfamiliar to her. The drummer was standing now, beating an ancient-looking wooden drum with a stick. The tune was rousing, and the locals were laughing and swaying to the music.

"It's a song in the Aleut language about a good fishing season of several years ago," came Ransom's explanatory whisper.

Disconcerted by his nearness, Sara shifted slightly and said, "It's very nice."

He nodded. "It's especially nice if you consider that when my mother was a child, she was forced to speak English. If she spoke Aleut she had to eat soap. Even so, she and her friends, would sneak off and talk it, anyway. It's nice to see a culture that was almost lost being brought back."

"Do you speak Aleut?" Sara asked in genuine interest.

"Sure." He cleared his throat and said something in a language she didn't understand, then gave her a smile that sent her pulses racing.

"What did you say?" she asked, unsure if she wanted to know.

"I said AT&T is up three-tenths of a point."

She countered doubtfully, "That's not what you said."

"Okay, my Aleut's a little rusty. Maybe I asked if you'd like to dance."

"It's not very flattering when a man isn't sure whether he asked you to dance or gave you a stock-market tip."

"I hadn't realized it was flattery you wanted from me," he murmured.

"Well, I, uh..." Words failed her. Ransom's eyes glistened with such tormenting allure that Sara lost her ability to protest, and her face grew fiery. It frightened her to realize how unnerving his glance could be, so she decided to make a quick exit before he could pull her into his arms.

Obviously anticipating her retreat, Ransom took her hand in his and drew her toward the span of beach used for a dance floor. As they took center stage, the Aleut fishing song faded away, somehow drifting into a very credible version of Buddy Holly's "True Love Ways."

Sara was filled with a confusing mixture of emotions—both dreadful hesitance and heady anticipation. The last time Ransom had taken her in his arms, he'd kissed her and sent her senses soaring, then stalked impatiently away. The memory flooded back in all its painful glory as he drew her close now, making her breathing quicken and become labored. Her embarrassment was so strong she couldn't meet his eyes. Instead, she focused on his muscular chest, swathed in red flannel and tried to calm herself. After all, they were only dancing!

The bonfires were ablaze, and Sara had removed her parka. She wore an oversize sweater that seemed suddenly stifling now that his arm was about her waist. Their bodies touching intimately, Ransom murmured, "Really, what I said in Aleut was 'The fog is lifting and tonight there will be stars.'"

A bit dazed, she explored the world around her and realized it was true. The fog had dwindled to nothing more than a few twisted, diaphanous fingers. Sometime before the dance was over, darkness would fall and there would be a clear, star-filled night.

Caught firmly in Ransom's embrace, she suppressed a shiver—not because her wool sweater allowed in any chill, but because she wasn't sure she could resist him under a sky full of twinkling stars. She hoped this local band of mature, responsible adults would avoid playing sexy ballads while Ransom held her in his arms. If not, Sara was very afraid she would be unable to reject the man who quietly regarded her with lazy seduction glittering in his eyes.

CHAPTER NINE

THE EVENING BECAME Sara's worst nightmare and fondest dream. Millions of years ago, stars gave off their cool, flawless light so that at this very minute their faraway shimmer would pay delicate homage to one particular man's lashes and the breeze-tossed gleam of his hair. What a cruel, yet wondrous coincidence, Sara thought, that she should be the one woman in the universe obliged to witness such perfection—and at this breathless proximity.

Ransom embraced her as they moved languidly to the mellow strains of "Red Sails in the Sunset." Driftwood bonfires burned low, flickering pleasantly. The wood smoke mingled with the briny tang of the sea and the crispness of the night, as the dying tongues of flame gently illuminated couples who lingered on the sand, swaying to the enduring love song.

Sara was dancing with her eyes closed, savoring the sensory pleasures of being in Ransom's arms. She could feel his strength as he moved against her. Taut, honed muscles that could easily crush her, held her with the lightness of a baby's kiss. His ever-taunting scent, a musky blend of cedar and leather, hovered about her, whispering bold promises of even more stimulating delights to come—if she was willing.

Ransom had acted like a perfect gentleman the whole evening, his gallant behavior lulling her into a sense of security. After all, they were in the midst of a crowd, all people he knew. What could he possibly do here? At long last, and after much inner turmoil, Sara gave up the vigilant fight and decided to trust him, succumbing to his easy charm.

She lay her cheek against the inviting flannel of his shirt and sighed, nuzzling ever so lightly. Though a faint voice in her brain nagged that this was a fool's paradise, she refused to heed it, relishing, instead, the heat of strong fingers splayed across her lower back, softly massaging away every ounce of lingering resistance.

"Sara," Ransom murmured near her ear.

"Hmm?" She made the sound through another sigh, not wanting to break the spell by opening her eyes.

"You are beautiful, you know."

Something intense flared through her body. Alarmed by the power of her reaction, her eyes snapped open to search his face. "W-what did you say?" she croaked.

She saw tenderness in his perusal and a hot ache swelled in her throat. Somewhere in the perimeters of her mind, she became aware that they'd moved away from the other dancing couples and were behind the bandstand, shrouded in darkness. The crowd seemed distant, and the music little more than a delicious backdrop to their own unfolding drama. Her skin prickled pleasurably as she sensed she was about to be kissed. *No,* logic cried. *He won't!* In breathless expectation, she could only stare up at him. He was surely only a hallucination that would fade into the night and desert her in the midst of her foolish fantasy.

He said nothing more as his rapt gaze continued to hold her captive. She had an overwhelming urge to be close to him—closer, much closer, than she had ever been to any man.

His eyes sparked with some primal emotion, taking Sara's breath away. A dizzying current of desire rushed through her, a desire she could no longer deny. In one mindless instant, she flung her arms about his neck. Trembling with need, hoping that she hadn't misread his expression and that he'd reject her, she lifted her lips in a wordless plea craving to know at least once more the fiery rapture of his kiss.

A shadow of contrary emotion swept across his face. Growling a low curse, he pulled her harshly, almost brutally to him, his mouth covering hers. The roughness of his kiss made her gasp, but she held on tightly, accepting both his anger and his passion. After a moment he became gentler, inviting more. They clung together, and she returned kiss for kiss, touch for touch, with reckless abandon.

Thunderstruck by her eager response, Sara moaned against his mouth, clutching at the soft hair at his nape. Light-headed, she was aware only of the soft demand of male lips, of thigh boldly touching hip, of powerful arms wound possessively around her. Nothing else mattered.

But soon, all too soon, Ransom groaned and drew his lips from hers. Sara's lashes fluttered heavily against his cheek, and she felt weak, overcome by his kiss. Not wanting the experience to end, she whimpered, "No..." and impulsively lifted her mouth to meet his again.

He moved his hands to her shoulders, holding her slightly away. "Sara, we can't."

Enveloped by a sense of loss, she focused on his face. Savage longing glistened in his eyes, but also a stricken look, one that made her bite off her cry to be crushed within his embrace, devoured by his loving. The reason he watched her with such guilty yearning suddenly came to her, and with a rush of compassion, she caressed his cleft chin, declaring brokenly, "Don't feel as though you've cheated on your wife, Ransom. I understand your guilt, but such thoughts are natural after—"

"I know you're trying to help," he interrupted, self-reproach staining his tone, "but you're wrong. I don't feel like I've cheated on Jill." His lip curled. "If only it was that neat and tidy."

She took a halting step backward. "I'm sorry...." she began, perplexed by his cryptic remark. His expression was one of silent anguish, and his jaw worked in agitation. At a loss, Sara watched as his eyes narrowed. Seconds ago she had been wrapped in his arms, and now he looked down at her as though she was the enemy.

Sorrow stabbed her heart, for she had just discovered what all those love songs meant—she'd become Ransom's woman, mind and body, heart and soul, from the moment their blistering kiss began. The tragic irony was that he clearly regretted his lapse.

"Tell me," she implored, "what did I do wrong?"

"Nothing," he replied hoarsely. "It was my doing. First to last." Pivoting, he muttered, "Forgive my weakness. It won't happen again."

As she watched him walk away—again!—his rejection held her immobile. She began to shiver as the chill of both the night and stark reality seeped into her bones. The music died and with it, some hopeful light went out inside Sara. For once having reveled in Ransom's embrace, she knew the most ardent caresses of other men would pale by comparison.

Sinking listlessly to the ashen sand, she hugged herself, feeling very alone. Ransom's final words echoed in her brain each time a wave broke on the shore its snakelike hiss taunting over and over, *It won't happen again. It won't happen again....*

SARA WORKED at the kitchen counter putting together a chicken casserole. It was six o'clock in the evening. Tag and Lynn had just left to go visit several other young people in the village. All morning and afternoon Sara and Ransom had sought refuge behind civil masks for the sake of the children. But now that the youngsters were gone, they were displaying their real feelings, and the atmosphere had gone icy. The house was deathly still but for the scrape of Sara's spoon against the mixing bowl and the occasional flip of a magazine page in the distance.

Ransom was in the living room, his feet propped up on the coffee table, apparently absorbed in a magazine. But he couldn't fool her. The pages were turning too rapidly for any real understanding, unless Ransom was a graduate of some speed-reading course.

Flip. Flip. Flip.

Sara rolled her eyes heavenward. Ransom had disposed of three pages in two seconds. Mr. Speed-read strikes again. She glanced at the cookbook and grimaced. Had she already put in the dash of curry? She hesitated, a teaspoon poised over the bowl. A little curry gave the dish zest. Too much made it appetizing only to die-hard curry lovers.

"Do you like curry?" she called coolly.

"No." His reply was equally crisp.

In an uncharacteristic surge of churlishness, she dumped the spice in. That would show Mr. It-won't-happen-again exactly how little she cared about him or his likes and dislikes.

He flipped another page, observing dryly, "I presume we're having curry for dinner."

"Curried chicken casserole."

"When exactly did it become *curried* chicken casserole?"

"About five seconds ago."

She heard the magazine slap onto the top of the coffee table. Next came the brisk stride of an angry man crossing the living room rug. She flinched when the hollow clomp of boots hitting the kitchen tile announced he was within strangling distance. Her body quivered because of his troublesome closeness, and she refused to face him. Instead, she began to chop an onion. It was a treacherous occupation, for the knife was razor sharp, and Ransom was standing all too near her for her hands to go unaffected. She rebuked herself for letting it matter, but she couldn't help it.

Her indifference was a transparent ruse, which she was sure he knew. And she was also sure he knew she was still smarting from his rejection on the beach.

"I told you I was sorry, Sara. What more can I do?" he asked, sounding provoked.

She chopped the onion into atoms, her teeth clenched to prevent her from telling him what she'd like to see him do—preferably in a hand basket!

"Aren't you even speaking to me?"

After scraping the onion bits into the mixing bowl, she slammed the cutting board down and shot him a baneful look. "Do not tempt me, Mr. Shepard. You might force me to utter words that dirty-mouthed thugs save for really bad days!"

Unwittingly she wielded her knife in his direction, and he took a prudent step backward. When she realized what she was doing, she banged it onto the counter with such force the cutting board rattled. "I'm not going to slice anything off, if that's what you're worried about," she grumbled.

"I'm grateful," he said almost gently. "But I wouldn't blame you after the way I behaved last night."

Her chest tightened, and she found herself mute. Unable to look at him, knowing her face must be bright red, she began to frantically stir the contents of the mixing bowl.

"You were so lovely, I..."

She stirred as though demons had possessed her wooden spoon.

"I'm a lonely man, Sara. You're beautiful and warm and, well—" his voice was almost a whisper "—I'm only human. I'd told myself I wouldn't kiss you again—not ever." He chuckled bitterly. "But ever since the first time I did..."

Her mad stirring slowed on its own. She waited almost without breathing, erratically moving the spoon around, her mind wholly on the gaping space left when his sentence had faded away. Her lips thinned. She'd be darned if she'd ask, but her mind cried, *Ever since the first time you did, what happened?*

When the casserole was mixed, she heaped it into a loaf pan and shoved it into the oven. Stifling the impulse to return to his side, she did her best to ignore him, tossing utensils into the sink and running water over them.

"Sara," he said regretfully, "I was wrong to kiss you. But, damn, you're one exciting woman."

She faltered with her scrub brush, but tried to hide it by redoubling her efforts to scour the mixing bowl. Though she feigned disinterest, all five of her senses, every cell of her body, were zeroed in on his words.

"You taste wonderful, and I'm angry with myself for liking it," he said, his voice thick. "I don't plan to—" He cut himself off with a raw curse. "Forgive me, Sara. That's all I have to give you."

His clipped footfalls receded rapidly. As soon as she was sure he was gone, she let out the breath she'd been holding and her body seemed to become boneless. At least Ransom had shown some decency by not reminding her that *she'd* been the one to fling herself into his arms last night. Even so, they both knew who'd kissed whom. A shudder of humiliation ran through her at the memory, and she clutched desperately at the sink's rim, hating herself for her stupidity.

Two hours later, the four of them sat in silence, each enduring the spicy casserole, in his or her own way. Tag was stirring his portion into his rice and peas, eating very little. Sara noticed that every few seconds he'd dart a nervous glance toward his father. It seemed that rather than being put off by the dinner, Tag had some other problem weighing heavily on his mind. She inspected him discreetly, wondering what the boy was fretting about.

Ransom cleared his throat, and Sara's gaze skittered his way. He'd graciously managed to finish his entire serving without complaint. Sara hated to do it, but she had to give him credit. He *was* attempting to make amends for rejecting her.

Trying to get her mind off Ransom, Sara said, "Tag, you and Lynn have been awfully quiet this evening." She smiled first at Tag, who was at the end of the table to Ransom's left, and then at Lynn, to the right. "Anything wrong?"

The boy gulped repeatedly. Lynn eyed Tag sympathetically. Worried she'd said the wrong thing, Sara balled her hands in her lap, hoping whatever the problem was, it could be solved easily.

"Say, Dad," Tag said, sounding timid, "I was talking to some of the kids this afternoon and I was... I was thinking maybe I could go to high school in Anchorage next year instead of Seattle. And this summer, after you go back to work, I could... I could maybe live at home with you and maybe work at the—"

"I don't think so, Tag," Ransom cut in, his features darkening into a scowl. "The Kirkwood Academy is an excellent school. I want you to continue your education there."

Tag reddened. "But I *hate* that school. I want to go home and live with you."

Fury flashed in Ransom's eyes, and he abruptly stood. "I don't intend to discuss it with you, Taggart. The matter's settled." His sudden departure was followed by a difficult stillness.

Sara felt badly for the boy, but didn't know what to say. His face was screwed up in an effort not to cry. "Why...?" Tag began brokenly, then clearing his throat, tried again. "Why can't he love me?"

His unhappiness was so acute it was like a slap. Sara hurried over to him. Kneeling beside his chair, she wrapped her arms about him. "Oh, Tag, he loves you. He's just having a hard time getting over your mother's death. You're his son—he can't help but love you."

Breaking free of her comforting embrace, he charged, "He hates me!" Tears streaking his cheeks, he choked out, "I know he hates me!" When he lunged away, his chair fell backward. Its clattering impact was followed speedily by the slamming of the front door.

With a heavy sigh, Lynn, too, got up. "I'd better go to him."

Sara nodded. "He probably needs a friend right now."

At the kitchen door, Lynn stopped and peered at her sister. "Tag was real scared of this," she confided. "I don't understand why Rance is being such a hard case. Do you?"

Lynn was gone before Sara could respond. But even if her sister had waited for an answer, Sara didn't know what she could have said. Righting Tag's chair, she sat down, feeling emotionally drained. Something was very wrong here. Ransom could be such a warm, easygoing person. His kiss had not been the kiss of an uncaring man. So why was he acting this way toward his son?

Although it wasn't her turn to clean up, she mindlessly cleared the table and washed the dishes pondering the problem. Why did Ransom seem to hate his own child? That was impossible, of course. Sara had seen the framed family portrait over his bed. Ransom Shepard loved his family. It was his wife's death that ate at him, not hatred for his son—although it was clear he didn't want much to do with Tag. Maybe the boy looked so much like his mother that seeing him was painful for Ransom. But that was no excuse to virtually abandon his own flesh and blood to the care of strangers.

She sat at the table for a long time, wondering if, after five years, his problem could still be all-consuming grief over his wife's death. Lilly had said he'd been completely devoted to Jill, and Sara had heard of people who never got over the loss of a spouse.

Then a thought struck her. What about that awkward moment after their kiss on the beach, when she'd thought he'd been guilt-ridden about betraying his wife's memory? He'd told her he didn't feel as if he'd cheated on Jill. So, if it wasn't grief and guilt, then what troubled him?

The clanging of a distant bell shattered the tense quiet like a gong being pounded near a sleeping person's ear. Sara jumped so sharply she almost upended the chair at second time.

Never having heard the sound before, she hurried to the front door. What could it mean? She glanced at her watch. It was nearly ten. As she went out on the porch steps to look around, she heard the thunder of boots behind her. Instinctively she slid out of the way as Ransom bounded across the threshold and headed toward town in a dead run.

"What's wrong?" she called.

"Emergency. Fishing boat's in trouble," he shouted back.

"Can I help?" she cried, but it was too late. He was out of earshot.

As she was struggling into a parka, both Lynn and Tag raced onto the porch. "We're going to help," panted Tag. "See you later."

"Oh, no, you don't," Sara retorted, dragging on her coat. "I'm going, too. I can help."

"Bring coffee," yelled Tag.

This stopped Sara. Of course. Whatever the problem was, there would be people in need of warmth when it was all over. "Then you two get blankets," she commanded.

They skidded to a halt several yards from the house, staring at each other. Without a word, they spun around and returned to the house. "Yeah, good idea," Tag said in the same clipped, authoritative tone his father often used. "You get the blankets from the hall closet, Lynn. I'll get towels."

By the time they'd bundled the bedding and towels in an old shower curtain, Sara had filled a thermos with coffee. Jogging along the hillside with them, she asked between breaths, "What do you suppose has happened?"

"Fishing boat's gone down, and they're gonna look for survivors."

"Oh, no!" Sara glanced at the ocean. It heaved like a thrashing dragon, and the wind was beginning to gust enough to even buffet them about.

"The village has a rescue boat, and it'll be light for two, two and a half more hours," Tag was explaining. "They've never lost anybody yet. We'll get 'em in okay."

When the trio reached the small deep-water harbor, the dock was teeming with villagers. The rescue boat, a scarred old powerboat with an observation tower, was being readied by a crew of able-bodied men and teenage boys.

Sara saw Ransom untying the bow. As the boat's engine sputtered fitfully to life, several native youths scrambled aboard.

Tag dropped his bundle on the wood planks of the dock and headed toward the craft, only to be stopped by Ransom.

Sara wasn't close enough to make out what they were saying, but she knew an argument was going on. As she neared, she could hear, "But Dad, other guys my age are going to help."

"You don't live here," Ransom said sternly. "These boys have grown up with the sea. I don't have time to debate with you, Tag. You're not going."

Ransom leapt over the gunwale and charged up the ladder to the fly bridge just as the rescue boat chugged away from the dock. Sara watched sadly as Tag's shoulders sagged, his hands going to his face in shame at his father's public rejection.

Seconds later, a driving rain began to fall. Sara found out from several of the villagers that two of their open fishing boats had been swamped by an unexpected swell that swept three men overboard. One of the men had been rescued by a third fishing boat, but two others were still out there in the hostile sea. The cold rain turned the attempted rescue into an oppressive, nail-biting business for those who could only stand on shore and peer hopefully out over the surging water.

Sara and Lilly huddled together holding a waterproof tarp about them. Lilly's husband, Dan, was one of the fishermen still missing. Having been offered a couple of folding chairs, they sat in silence, not knowing what to say. Lilly's toddler, Danny, squirmed unhappily in his mother's lap, hampered by the warm confines of one of the blankets Tag and Lynn had brought.

"More coffee, Lilly?" Sara asked, fumbling beneath the tarp for the thermos.

Lilly shook her head, staring blankly.

Wiping stinging rain from her eyes, Sara frowned, feeling helpless. She, too, watched the wild sea, praying the rescue would be successful and cursing the rain.

She thought she saw something ghostly begin to emerge from the gray storm. "Is that the boat?" she cried weakly.

Lilly, her hair plastered to her pretty, pinched face nodded. Apparently she'd already seen it, but said nothing. What was there to say, after all?

Almost afraid to hope, they watched as it approached. After what seemed like a lifetime, it docked, and two men lumbered over the gunwale with a burden on a stretcher.

"It's not Dan," Lilly whispered stoically.

She was right. The man was a twenty-six-year-old bachelor named Gabriel. He was suffering from hypothermia and a gash on his head.

As soon as the injured fisherman was safely on land, the boat headed out again. Lilly lowered her head and closed her eyes. With a lump welling in Sara's throat, she hugged the woman and soothed, "They'll find him. Don't worry, they'll find him." But they both knew time was running out.

A few minutes later Lynn ran up. She was the image of a soaked urchin from the streets, and her face was drawn with worry. "Where's Tag?" she asked breathlessly. "I've looked everywhere."

Foreboding crept up Sara's spine. "I thought he was with you."

Lynn shook her head, her stringy hair flapping in her eyes. "No. He told me he had to do something. Sara, I'm afraid...."

"Afraid of what?" Grasping her little sister by the shoulders, she asked, "What do you know?"

Lynn burst into tears, filling Sara with dread. "What?" she repeated, really frightened now.

A dazed look of helplessness spread over Lynn's face as she sobbed, "He...he... There was this rowboat, and Tag said he had to help, and now...now the boat's..."

"...gone," Sara finished, as terror settled over her like a shroud.

CHAPTER TEN

THE GALE RAGED ON. Yet, no matter how destructive the weather, neither Sara nor Lilly could be budged from their vigil on the rose-hued roadway that bordered the harbor. Both Lilly's husband and Ransom's son were missing on the savage Bering Sea.

A worried neighbor named Pat had finally convinced Lilly to let her put little Danny to bed in her house, not far away. Lynn had taken refuge on the porch of another family, though she continued to sob uncontrollably.

Using the radio in the one fishing boat that was still in commission, villagers tried to contact the rescue craft to let the men know about Tag. But the batteries were too weak to penetrate the stormy atmosphere, and they got nothing for their frantic efforts except squawking static.

The mood in the town was dismal as people milled helplessly about the dock and the roadside beyond, drenched and shivering. Sara's thermos was long empty, but from time to time village women passed among the watchers with mugs of hot coffee and soup. Through the rain, the glow of lighted windows could be seen all over town, for none but the smallest of children were going to get any sleep tonight. Two of their island brothers were missing at sea and after all this time, many whispered, were surely lost.

Sara hunched worriedly beside Lilly, her eyes trained on the darkening water. Still wrapped in the blanket and tarp, she tried to ward off another bout of shivers and a growing urge to burst into tears. Fearing the worst, Lilly had given up her stoic pose and now cried softly. Unsure how to help, Sara patted the young woman's hand beneath the tarp they shared.

They both knew there was little left to say. Dan had been in the ocean for more than an hour. The cold would have sapped his strength beyond his ability to stay afloat by now—unless he'd managed to climb onto something. And that possibility was unlikely.

Nevertheless, Sara closed her eyes and mouthed a silent prayer that somehow Dan was surviving, maybe at this very minute being ferried back to safety on the rescue boat. She'd only met the man once, last night at the festival, but she vividly recalled his skillful guitar playing, his hearty laugh and his penchant for knock-knock jokes. He'd been so cute with his little boy. It was obvious the husky fisherman loved his family, his work and his Aleut heritage.

Sara shook her head, amazed it had been only yesterday she'd met him. How ironic that now she waited to learn if he was to live or die before another day dawned. She shivered again, peering out at the stormy water. "Let him be all right," she murmured, wiping rain and welling tears from her eyes.

She couldn't even allow herself to think of Tag as being anything other than safe aboard his little rowboat. It was true that much larger boats than his had been swamped and overturned tonight, but she had to believe Tag would survive and be found. He was just a child—a likable, troubled boy who wanted nothing more than his father's love and acceptance. With a tremulous sigh, she added a prayer for the boy, hoping he would return on his own before Ransom even had to know he'd been missing.

Lilly jumped to her feet, their shared tarpaulin half dragging Sara with her. "The boat!" Lilly exclaimed in a forlorn cry, then ran toward the dock.

Sara could see it now, too. Dim lights flickered amid the tempest, pale and diaphanous proof the rescue boat was chugging into the harbor. She threw the tarp over the two folding chairs and charged after Lilly, her throat closing with fear and hope.

Rain battered the crowd that surged onto the wharf as the craft maneuvered into position at the dock. Before it was tied up, several men and boys jumped from the gunwale to the wooden planks. One of the first off was Ransom. He spotted Lilly and grabbed her hands. Sara was close behind the young woman and was shocked to see how haggard Ransom looked. He was soaked to the skin, his hair plastered to his face. And there was a ragged cut on his cheek.

Lilly said nothing and neither did Ransom for a long moment, then he took her gently into his arms. "We'll keep trying. We won't give up. I promise," he said consolingly, but his tone held anger and frustration. "We've got to take on more fuel," he explained. "And we're going to switch crews. Some of the men are pretty cold."

Giving her a quick hug, he urged, "Go and get a little rest."

Lilly's neighbor Pat came up and put an arm about her. "Come to my house and have a bite of food. You can see the dock from my kitchen window." Her face vacant and dazed, Lilly allowed herself to be drawn away.

Sara knew the time had arrived to tell Ransom about Tag. Filled with dread, she croaked, "Ransom..."

His glance snapped from Lilly's receding form to her anxious face. He saw the expression for what it was, and his frown grew more troubled. "What is it?" he asked.

Her anguish almost overcame her control, but she fought the sobs that blocked her throat and said, "It's Tag." She swallowed, unable to go on.

"What about Tag?" he asked. Even with the storm raging about them, his question had been almost too quiet.

"He's...he wanted to help," she said, the knowledge of what her words would do to Ransom twisting her insides.

His expression turned grim as he watched her. When she didn't go on, he asked harshly, "What did he do?"

"He took out a rowboat. Nearly an hour ago..."

Ransom shuddered visibly and drew a sharp breath. "Lord, no," he moaned, his breathing becoming harsh. Spinning away, he started to leap aboard the boat.

Sara lunged forward, grabbing his hand. "Ransom, you can't go now. You're soaked to the skin and your cheek—it's bleeding."

"Like hell I can't," he shouted. "I've got to go. He's my..." His voice faltered, and he flinched as though someone had punched him in the gut. Staggering slightly, his shoulders sagged; he was clearly near exhaustion.

She tangled her fingers with his, admonishing, "You're not fit. You're cold and you're hurt. You must go up to the house and at least change into dry clothes. I'll doctor that cut. By the time we're done, I'm sure they'll have found both Dan and Tag. If not..." She looked away from the pain glimmering in his eyes, not wanting to think about that possibility. Hurriedly she added, "Well, then you'll be in better shape to go back out yourself."

They both knew the odds of finding either Tag or Dan in this weather were slim. It had gone unsaid, but even Sara understood that a rescue effort in this gale was not only fairly hopeless, but also foolhardy. There was a chance that some of the rescuers could be injured or killed going out on the ocean in a decrepit boat in this storm. But no man was willing to be the first to say the effort was useless or foolish. These man were seasoned fisherman, and they were not going to let a friend die without giving their all in an attempt to save him.

Ransom shot a glance at the bobbing powerboat as a fresh crew boarded. His jaw working, he agreed, "I'll change, but let's not waste any time."

As he loped toward his home, Sara detoured to the house where Lynn had taken shelter. Her younger sister had fallen into a fitful sleep on the porch, and they'd covered her with a blanket. She looked too fragile to be awakened into this unhappy reality, so Sara thanked the family and told them she'd be back to fetch her later.

When she got to Ransom's, she was breathing hard and soaked through. Stripping off her sopping parka, she went inside to find he had changed into dry jeans and a bulky turtleneck.

Sara grabbed a towel and wrapped it around her wet hair. "Give me a second to change, and I'll get medicine for that cut," she told Ransom. "You go sit on the couch."

A scant minute later, having thrown on dry clothes and grabbed up some medical supplies, she went into the living room and found it empty. She feared he'd gone back to the dock. As she was about to run to the hall closet to look for a dry coat, she heard a sound in the kitchen.

With a sigh of relief, she followed the noise and dropped her first-aid things on the table. "Let me fix that cut, Ransom."

He was spooning fresh coffee grounds into the percolator. "Thought I'd take hot coffee to the dock," he said, sounding tired.

She sat down. "Good idea. But before you go, why don't you have a cup to warm yourself?"

He plugged in the pot and faced her. His features were drawn, his eyes haunted. "If Tag dies," he muttered, "I don't think I'll ever be warm again."

She couldn't meet those eyes, they were so full of agony. She lowered her gaze to her hands, which she twisted anxiously in her lap. Clearing her throat, she said, "Let me fix your face. They said they'd ring the bell if the rescue boat returned before you got there."

He moved toward her with a heavy tread. Though the kitchen was toasty warm, the chill of despair dwelt there with them, and she shuddered.

A chair scraped. She looked his way as he sat down. Ransom said nothing, and she watched him in misery.

"Just fix the damned cut," he muttered, clearly not wanting her pity.

Fumbling with the gauze, antiseptic and tape, she became distracted by his face, his sharp-edged masculinity, handsome even in its bleakness. "How did you cut yourself?" she asked, trying to get her mind on her task.

"One of the boys went up in the observation tower. The water was too rough and he fell. When I dove for him, I caught the safety rail with my face."

"How's the boy?"

"Wiser." Grimly he added, "I wish I could say the same for myself."

Soaking a piece of gauze with antiseptic, she grazed his chin with a finger to indicate a need to have him turn slightly. When he did, their eyes met. His glance was direct, almost challenging. She was hard put not to ask him what he was thinking.

He didn't flinch when the medicated gauze touched his torn flesh, but Sara knew it wasn't a shallow desire to appear macho. More likely, he'd simply gone numb with worry over his son's plight, and felt nothing as paltry as physical pain.

After cleaning the wound, she applied a dressing. "There. That should be fine. I don't think you'll need stitches."

"You have a light touch, Sara," he said, though his tone was flinty.

"I—I've always wanted to be a nurse."

His nostrils flared. "Dammit. Be a nurse, then. Life's too short."

Suddenly he slammed both his fists on the tabletop and vaulted to his feet. "Blast my hide! What have I done?" he bellowed, toppling his chair as he stormed from the room.

Shocked, Sara hurried after him, assuming he was about to bolt headlong down to the dock. But when she ran into the living room, he was standing there, leaning heavily against the stone mantelpiece. On the hearth, the driftwood fire flickered weakly.

Seeing this big strong man so inconsolable was heartrending, and tears slowly found their way down her cheeks. Not caring how it would look, or if it was right or wrong, she went to him and slid a comforting arm about his waist. "This wasn't your fault, Ransom."

His muscles tensed beneath her fingers. "I wish it wasn't."

Wanting to help him through his torment, she said, "I know you and Tag had a fight before you left, and I know you're thinking if only you hadn't been short with him...."

He grasped her roughly by the arms. "No, Sara, no!" he countered harshly. "That's not at all what I'm thinking." Though he never raised his voice, each word quivered with self-loathing. "I'm thinking about how I tried for five years to hate that boy, and now, when I have to face the fact that he might be—" to Sara's dismay, his voice broke "—that he might be dead, I find I can't do it. I love him, dammit. And it's too late to tell him so."

"Hate?" she echoed disbelievingly.

He released her. "It's not a pretty word, is it?" he asked, his voice harsh with emotion.

She shook her head.

His lips twisted into a parody of a smile. "Sweet Sara. Sweet, responsible Sara who wants to be a nurse. She can't understand why a man would try to hate his own son."

He crossed to the couch and dropped down onto it, running his hands distractedly through his hair. "Hell, why won't this rain let up?" he groaned.

"It...it's only been a few minutes since we got here," she reminded him. "The coffee will take at least five more minutes to perk. Just try to relax." Feeling powerless, she trailed after him and sat down by him, urging, "I think you need to talk, Ransom. Something's been eating at you for a long time."

He darted a mutinous look her way, and in it, Sara witnessed the shadow of his sadness and its vile complexity, raw and very close on the surface. Somehow she knew that, tonight, he was going to tell her things he'd kept bottled up for years. Needing to help him on his difficult journey, she took one of his large, restless hands in both of hers and implored, "Talk to me, Ransom."

The rain on the roof sounded like machine-gun fire as Sara waited. He needed to do this in his own time, so no matter how disturbed she was, no matter how knotted her stomach was, she'd wait.

He leaned forward, propping his chin on his other hand. His eyes were closed, his lips drawn in a fierce line. After a nerve-racking moment, he faced her.

"I told you once I had no brother," he said, his voice cold.

She nodded, disconcerted by his savage scrutiny.

"I had a brother once, but now he's dead."

Sara forced herself not to ask questions. He had to tell the story in his own way.

"His name was Morgan, and he was three years older than I. In college, he dated Jill for a while, but married another girl."

Ransom dropped his gaze and seemed to go inward, backwards, to some distant time. "I'd always liked Jill. One day we bumped into each other on campus, and things moved along pretty fast. Within a month we were married." He paused for a moment before he said, "She had a difficult pregnancy. Tag was premature, and the doctor said she couldn't have any more children. That didn't matter to me. Taggart and Jill were enough."

Sara knew he'd been a happy husband and father. Why, then was there such a bitter edge to his words?

"Five years ago," he went on stonily, "I came home from work to find a note from Jill telling me she'd run off with Morgan. It went on to explain that she'd been furious about Morgan's marriage to another woman. So, out of spite, she'd planned our chance meeting. Knowing I had a crush on her, she'd used that fact to her advantage."

Ransom's hand tightened around Sara's and she winced, but that was more from sympathy than from pain.

"Jill was very good at her scheming," he said gravely. "I never knew she wanted Morgan back until he finally left his wife, and he and Jill ran away together."

Ransom met Sara's widened eyes and flashed a humorless grin. "You look almost as miserable as I felt. But that's not the worst of it." He shook his head, continuing in a subdued voice, "She also wrote that she'd send for Taggart in a week or two—after the honeymoon. *My son.*" He clenched his jaw, obviously fighting for control. "You've probably guessed the rest by now. Jill and Morgan were killed on an icy highway near Anchorage. But her coup de grace was written out for me to read and reread until I wanted to go blind rather than accept the truth."

Tugging his shaking hand from Sara's, he rubbed it across his mouth. What he was about to say was being wrenched from the deepest, darkest part of his soul. Sara stirred uneasily, wanting to take him in her arms, but she held back. *Let him say it!* her mind warned. *Let him get it out. The pain of doing that will cauterize the wound.*

When he twisted toward her, his features were grave. As though the words were covered with spines and being ripped out of his gut, he rasped, "Jill told me that the son I adored wasn't even mine—he was Morgan's."

A huge, gaping hole was blown through Sara's heart with those words, and she had an urge to scream out her anger at the woman who'd hurt this man so horribly, but she held herself in check, allowing Ransom to finish.

"Jill confessed that she'd found herself pregnant with my brother's baby, but he'd refused to leave his wife for her. So, she planned revenge on him and married me." He gave a bitter smile. "When Tag was born, I suppose she thought she was paying Morgan back by insisting we give his child my name—Tag's full name is Ransom Taggart Shepard."

"I can't imagine anyone doing something so malicious and cruel," Sara breathed.

"I couldn't, either," he said, his eyes dark with pain.

"She might have been lying," Sara offered hopefully.

"That's what I hoped at first. I refused to believe her, but blood tests proved her right." His glance shifted away and he seemed to be staring at nothing in particular. "I finally had to face it." His voice hollow, he said, "Tag isn't my son."

Sara's heart bled for him, and she clutched her hands to her breast, horrified by the ugly revelation. She was doubly horrified that she'd ever accused this man of shirking his duties as a parent. Hearing that must have been like having hot coals thrust in his eyes.

"So, you went a little crazy and sent him away, and tried to hate him for what his deceitful mother did to you," Sara offered gently. "But you couldn't hate an innocent child, could you?"

Ransom turned his gaze to the ceiling. "I gave it one hell of a try, shipping him off to a private school in another state, never visiting him, drowning my anger in work." He laughed shortly, but his eyes glimmered with sorrow. "Got damned rich working day and night. Damned rich and damned miserable."

"How did you come to be with him this summer?" Sara asked.

Ransom shrugged powerful shoulders. "He was suffering. I knew it but tried not to care. He got into fights, did some petty vandalism. His grades were dismal. The academy told me if he didn't shape up they'd expel him." A look of weary sadness crossed his features. "Tag has no one else. So, I brought him here—not knowing he'd been planning to find me a wife. I imagine he thought if I married again, things would be like they were before."

"Poor kid," Sara mused, trying to control the rage she had for Jill. The selfish woman had done two wonderful people so much damage. And Tag, Jill's blameless son, might pay for her subterfuge with his life.

Sara's vision clouded with tears. Ashamed, she whispered, "Oh, Ransom, I called you names, when you were trying to do the decent thing, trying to help the boy, even though..." A sob broke from her throat and she pressed her lips together to steady their trembling. "I'm so sorry...." she managed wretchedly.

"You couldn't have known," he said.

Their glances met. Somehow Sara found herself in Ransom's arms, his lips touching hers like a whisper. The passion of the other evening was tempered mightily by tonight's tragic events. But this time they shared an honesty that was, to Sara, much more desirable and memorable than yesterday's heart-stopping kiss. The fondness, the caring in his caress now awakened in her new, pure love for him, and her heart hammered with reaction. When their lips parted, she gazed at him and sighed tremulously. "I'm glad you told me everything."

His countenance grim, Ransom drew away from her, though she sensed his reluctance. "The rain's stopped," he murmured, rising to his feet. "I'm going back."

She nodded in understanding, wishing she didn't feel as limp as a dishrag, wishing she'd never seen this unguarded side of Ransom. For now she was even more hopelessly in love with him than before. At least she knew why he'd resisted love all these years—he didn't trust himself to know honest affection when it stared him in the face. Since he'd been duped by Jill, he'd rejected possible relationships out of hand, to protect his heart from more such damage.

She pushed herself up to stand beside him. This was a poor time to torture herself with the realization that she loved a man who was afraid to love, afraid to trust. Besides, the lives of two people were at risk, and the search was still on. Dragging the towel from her hair, she offered, "I'll put the coffee in the thermos and—"

There was a reverberating crash nearby, and they both spun to discover its cause. Sara's first thought was that a gust of wind had blown the door open, but when she saw what had actually happened, her mouth fell open in astonishment.

"Tag!" they exclaimed in unison.

The boy was slumped against the doorjamb, drenched and quaking with cold. He was holding his hands in an odd, cramped way, and Sara could see blood on his palms.

They hurried over to help him to the couch, but he struggled to be free, protesting hoarsely, "No. Gotta help—in the cove..."

"Cove?" Ransom repeated.

"D-Dan..."

That one unsteady response sent a bolt of white-hot hope zinging through Sara, and she tried, "You've got Dan in a cove? In your rowboat?"

Tag nodded.

"What cove, Tag?" Ransom urged.

"Sea...sea..."

"Sea Lion Cove?"

Tag nodded again, smiling faintly.

Ransom was staring at Tag, his expression one of amazement, but his eyes were filled with love and pride. Sara knew her features mirrored his. It was astounding, almost miraculous, but apparently this trembling, slight boy had actually rescued Dan from sure death.

Ransom's mouth worked wordlessly. There was so much to say, but now was not the same. Sara watched Ransom's handsome face as he experienced a gamut of emotions, then after only the briefest hesitation he grabbed the boy in a bear hug. A telltale glisten in his expressive gray eyes spoke volumes. "Oh, thank God. Son..." He said the word tentatively at first, as though testing the idea. "Son," he whispered through a ragged groan, "I thought you were..."

Shakily the boy dragged his arms up to encircle his father's broad body. "Sorry, Dad... but I had to."

Ransom stepped back, relief softening his haggard features. "Don't talk now." He smiled. "Rest and get warm. I'll find Dan. Sara—"

"I'm on my way," she called, running to the porch and grabbing a dry coat from a hook. "I'll tell Lilly and get Doc Stepetin."

As she buttoned up, she heard Tag insist, "I've got to go, Dad. I've got—"

Ransom cut him off. "I can see you've inherited my stubbornness, Taggart. Come on."

They raced past her into the darkness—a father and his son. Sara had detected fierce pride in Ransom's voice just now and realized the rift between them was healed at last.

She gloried in the precious moment she'd been privileged to witness and knew she would treasure this memory long after both Ransom and Tag had forgotten her existence.

Sara's euphoric mood was crushed with that stinging reminder. It was true. Ransom and Tag would forget her, for the man she loved would not learn to trust a woman again, not without a long struggle. By that time, she would no longer be a part of his life. That was a hard reality, but one she had to face—and soon—for she'd be leaving St. Catherine Island in three days. Sobered by the thought, she ran out into the overcast, dying day.

CHAPTER ELEVEN

HALF THE TOWN returned to the house with Sara when the news spread of Dan's amazing rescue by the fourteen-year-old boy. And Tag, though bathed in smiles, was a hesitant, tired hero. Dan was exhausted and cold but happy to be alive. After a tearful reunion with his wife and son, a hundred hands helped transport him back to Doc's place for treatment.

Forty minutes later, Lynn, her eyes still red-rimmed from crying, was in the kitchen making cocoa. She hummed off-key, but it was a welcome sound. Ransom stoked the fire with more driftwood, making the room cheery after the night's near disaster.

Tag, wrapped in a robe, sat on the couch while Sara bandaged his thin hands, torn and raw from rowing.

When Lynn carried in a tray containing four steaming mugs, she said, "Why's everybody so quiet? I want to know what happened." Settling the tray on the coffee table, she gave Tag a cup.

He took it awkwardly with one bandaged hand. "Like I told Doc," he began, his throat raspy, "saving Dan was pretty much an accident. It was raining bad, and I wasn't even rowing, just trying not to overturn, when I saw this white thing coming at me on a swell. When it got about five feet away, I saw it was Dan, hanging on to a plastic cooler, and I yelled. He saw me and grabbed for an oar."

Tag took a sip of cocoa. "Dan's smart, knows boats better'n me, so he knew how to get in real careful. We almost tipped a couple of times, but he finally made it in. I'd brought along a blanket wrapped in that old shower curtain, so I put the blanket around him and laid the plastic on top to keep him warm. By then he didn't have enough strength to do more than just lie there and shiver. He was pretty tired, too tired to even talk."

"So, you rowed until you saw land?" Sara asked, patting his hand to let him know she was finished bandaging it.

He grinned sheepishly. "Nah. I couldn't see anything in that storm. I was afraid to row 'cause I thought I'd take us out to sea. So I didn't do anything for a long time but hold on. Then—" he paused and frowned "—I heard this noise—sounded kinda like mechanical laughter. Weird. After a minute I saw Potluck. He was alongside my boat stickin' his snout out, waggin' it, trying to get my attention."

"The dolphin?" Ransom asked, taking a seat next to his son on the couch.

"Yeah. He acted like he wanted to play."

"You mean the hat game?" Lynn asked, eyes wide.

Tag nodded. "I thought he was nuts. I was having all kinds of problems just trying to keep the boat steady. I was freezing and lost and that stupid fish wanted to play."

"It's not a fish, dork, it's a mammal." Lynn obviously couldn't resist teasing Tag. "I keep telling ya—"

"Whatever," Tag cut her off with a smirk. "Anyway, I yelled at the *mammal* to leave me alone, but he kept on squeaking at me. Finally I quit being so dumb, and I figured it out."

"What?"

"How Potluck could help me find land."

"You threw him your ball cap," Ransom guessed, smiling.

Tag nodded again, returning the smile timidly. "It worked. I'd lose sight of him a lot, 'cause I couldn't row very fast, but that crazy fish, er, mammal kept coming back to me with my cap in his snout."

"What a smart dolphin," Sara mused aloud. "It's almost as though he was trying to help."

"You think?" Tag asked, taking another sip of cocoa.

"It doesn't really matter," Ransom answered. "But I, for one, am donating to Save the Dolphin from now on."

"Me, too," gushed Lynn. "I wonder if Potluck knows he saved two human lives tonight?"

Tag shrugged. "I don't care if he knows or not. But that's the way *I'm* telling it." Then he yawned. "But it wasn't today. It was yesterday. It's dark outside, so it must be tomorrow."

"Tag's right," Sara said, gathering together the first-aid gear. "He needs to get to bed. We all should."

The boy stood up shakily, cradling his injured hands to his chest. As he began to move toward the hallway, Ransom got up, too. "I'll bring your lantern in later, Tag."

"Okay, Dad." Tag averted his eyes, mumbling. "Sorry about being a butt."

Ransom's grin was rueful. "I think that's my line." Dropping an arm about his son's shoulders, he said, "I've failed you in a lot of ways, Taggart. I hope I can make it up to you."

Tag looked up at his father, his face the picture of awe. The only sound that intruded on the precious moment was the crackling of the fire. Tag uncurled one of his injured hands and put it on his father's shoulder. "You're only human, Dad," he replied, patting the big man. "We all make mistakes."

They disappeared into the hallway leaving Sara and Lynn sitting there holding cooling mugs of cocoa. When the sisters glanced at each other, both pairs of hazel eyes were shiny with tears.

THE REMAINDER of Sara's stay had passed all too quickly. The villagers had dropped by often with little gifts of thanks. Lilly brought a quart each of blackberry and moss-berry jam. Other villagers brought breads, smoked meats, pies and cakes, so much, in fact, there'd hardly been any need to cook.

Tag bore his heroism with remarkable poise. Sara believed he knew he'd done a stupid thing and had only lived because of good fortune. Nevertheless, all the attention showered on their house made the ensuing couple of days fly by.

Tag and Ransom had become as close as a father and son could be, making up for lost time. Sara was gratified to hear that Tag would be going to school in Anchorage next fall and living with his father from now on.

Ransom's attitude toward Sara, however, had left much to be desired—at least as far as her heart was concerned. He was no longer angry with her, or glowering in her direction from between narrowed lashes. But when she caught his eye, his expression held a measure of regret and unease. She couldn't tell if he regretted revealing his unhappy secret to her and was uneasy because he feared she pitied him, or if there was some small part of him that regretted knowing she would soon be gone.

The second possibility was most likely her own heart talking. That was what *she* wanted him to be thinking. She wanted him to hate the idea that she would soon be out of his life. And her leaving would certainly mean that. After all, what possible reason would a salmon tycoon have to visit a landlocked state like Kansas? No reason whatsoever that she could think of, and she'd spent countless sleepless hours trying to come up with one.

Her fantasies, though, *did* have him needing to visit Kansas all the time—to see her. She would have laughed if it hadn't been so painful. To see her, indeed! And she knew the reason he wouldn't come wasn't because he was still grieving over his lost wife. He was brooding over his loss of trust. Jill's supposed devotion had been a complete lie—a lie he'd believed for nine years before she'd cruelly yanked his world from beneath him.

It was apparent he couldn't trust himself to love again. This knowledge had seemed to kill Sara's spirit. She'd walked around pretending to be alive, but she was numb all the way to her core. She felt as if she'd been sealed up in a cold dank tomb, never allowed to savor life to its fullest because the man she loved had lost the power to say, "I trust you with my heart." She couldn't blame or fault Ransom for his inability to reach out to her, though he must have sensed her love for him. Her feelings were glaringly evident in her voice, her manner, her every glance.

Looking down at her clenched hands, Sara rubbed the slight scar that remained from the time the dog had bitten her. Even after all these years she couldn't bring herself to trust dogs—or adorable foxes. Her mind still refused to allow her to offer her hand to even the sweetest-looking puppy. She imagined it must be even more difficult for Ransom, scarred so badly by a woman, to give his heart to another.

So she and Ransom had spent these last days sharing nothing but polite, meaningless conversation, his eyes warning that she follow his lead and make no comment about his revelation or her painfully exposed love for him.

Sara glanced at her watch. It was eleven o'clock Wednesday morning. Krukoff would be flying in at any moment. There was no wind, and the sky was clear and sunny. It was as though the whole Northern Hemisphere was conspiring with Ransom to get her off St. Catherine Island. She wiped away a tear as she took the last batch of hearty whole-grain bread from the oven. Her mind wailed, *Why couldn't this conspiracy between man, wind and weather have taken place a week ago?*

She might have recovered from the damage to her heart then. But not now. She would carry the memory of Ransom's kisses with her to old age, and any man who might one day try to compete with that memory would surely fail.

"The house smells good," Ransom said, coming up silently behind her.

She closed her eyes, savoring the rich sound of his voice. "Thank you," she murmured. Trying desperately to lighten the mood, she joked, "I hope you won't need a chain saw to cut this batch of bread."

"You didn't have to bake bread, Sara," he said coolly.

"It was the least I could do," she muttered. He hadn't reacted at all to her attempt at humor. It was ironic, she mused as she moved the loaves to a basket and covered them with a cloth. She'd continually scolded Ransom for his teasing and taunting only days ago. What she would have given right now for one of his devilish grins and a kidding remark about forklifts.

She was being silly, she knew, but she felt a shattering loss. Her whole being cried out to know this man intimately, to marry him and bear his children. For a few brief moments in his arms, she'd come close. He'd revealed himself to be a tender lover who could make her happy to simply be a woman. Yet now he treated her as if she was an aged schoolmarm or nun—with distant respect, but no familiarity. She knew, if given the choice, she would miss his playful affection more than she would miss breathing.

"All packed?" he asked, breaking into her sad reverie.

Trying not to show her distress over his aloof attitude, she nodded. "I've been packed for hours." Although she knew she would regret it, she turned toward him, then caught her breath. He was so tall and handsome, and his black hair was mussed just enough to make his face agonizingly endearing. She knew he hadn't planned on tormenting her, but he'd succeeded nevertheless.

His mouth tightened when their eyes met, and his eyebrows tilted downward. She couldn't decide if his harsh expression indicated annoyance or pity. Either one filled her with dismay.

"I'll get your bags," he offered. Her stomach contracted at his dispassionate tone, and she couldn't respond. There was an awkward pause before he asked, "Is Lynn packed?"

"She and Tag have already taken the bags to the airstrip," Sara said, grateful her voice didn't break.

"Oh." Another troublesome pause. "Then perhaps we should join them," he suggested, his face impassive.

How Sara hated this! She wanted to run into his arms, to ask him what she'd done that was so unforgivable he should put up such a harsh, impenetrable wall. Her only sin had been to listen and care—and love. How she missed the warm laughter in his gray eyes and the unceasingly wicked chuckle that had once infuriated her.

"You needn't bother going to the airstrip," she blurted, pride forcing her to pretend indifference through till the end. "You've done enough. Why don't you go do your egg count. I know it's important to you." She spun away to pick up the basket of bread and place it on top of the refrigerator, all the while aware of his scrutiny.

"A good host doesn't abandon his guests," he replied, his voice clipped.

She whirled on him. Unable to stop herself, she challenged, "I think we've gone beyond trivial social amenities, Ransom. Do what pleases you, for heaven's sake."

A flash of disquiet stole across his handsome face, but it was quickly replaced by that same infernal air of calmness. "Perhaps we have, Sara," he observed dryly. "I'll say goodbye here, then."

Cold dread engulfed her. This was it. She would never see him again. With courageous effort, she hid her despair behind a mask of politeness. "Goodbye. Thanks for your hospitality." She offered him a rigid hand to shake.

He flicked an insolent glance toward her outstretched fingers. "I thought we'd gone beyond trivial social amenities," he said, throwing her own words back at her.

With insulting deliberateness, he slid his hands into his hip pockets. This final rejection was simply too much. He wouldn't even touch her hand in a parting, if hollow, gesture of friendship. She blushed fiercely. How could he be so indifferent, so cold? How could she have thought he was a warm, caring person? Fearful that her torment and yearning lay naked in her eyes, Sara knew she must get away, must *run!* Damn her crumbling composure. If she didn't escape this instant, she'd be weeping in front of him, making more of a fool of herself than she already had.

Desolate, she rushed out of the kitchen, out of the house, and out of Ransom Shepard's life.

THE CHILLY NIP of the first day of February was in the crisp Kansas air. Sara inhaled the cool pine fragrance of the night. She exhaled and frosted the darkness with her warm breath. Standing under the half-hearted glow of the diner's fluorescent sign, she huddled deeper into her old wool coat and shivered. The bus was late again.

It didn't make much difference. Lynn was still at her after-school job, since the dress shop where she worked stayed open until nine on Thursdays. So, there'd be no one in the apartment, anyway. She might as well stand out here under the stars and enjoy the clean night air. She only wished that, just once this winter, it would snow. It hadn't yet, not once. Christmas had been dreary and bleak—but not because there hadn't been snow, she realized.

She hiked up her purse strap, regretting that she wouldn't be able to attend the community college again this semester. Finances were tight, and she would have to work. But she vowed to enroll this fall and keep at it until she graduated. She'd taken Ransom's angrily given advice. "Dammit, be a nurse!" he'd shouted at her.

When she'd returned to Kansas, she'd decided that was what she had to do. Besides, studying would help get her mind off a certain man back in Alaska.

First, she'd passed her high school equivalency test in August. Then, in September, she'd begun taking courses at Butler County Community College. Starting school again had been tough, working the breakfast and lunch shift at the diner and then going to class for three hours five nights a week. But she refused to feel sorry for herself. This was a dream she planned to make come true. Maybe she couldn't make *all* her dreams come true, but she'd succeed with this one, no matter how long it took!

She heard the bus roaring around the corner and walked to the curb, her mind slipping back to yesterday afternoon. Lynn had received another letter from Tag. He was doing well in school and was a member of the junior varsity basketball team. According to the letter, Ransom was an avid fan and never missed his son's games.

The door of the bus swooshed opened, and Ransom's sternly handsome face was pushed from her mind. She climbed aboard and took a seat beside Erma Drope, whom she almost always saw on the bus at night. The elderly woman was the town's most avid gossip, but Sara liked her, and greeted her with a smile.

Erma was the perfect image of a grandmother—plump, pink-cheeked and smelling of baking spices. Sara figured Erma must be close to a hundred, but each evening without fail, this four-times widowed woman took the bus to and from the local movie theater.

"What did you see this trip, Erma?" Sara asked, aware that as Erma's riding companion she was expected to inquire.

"Kurt's latest picture," Erma gushed, fluffing her wispy white hair.

"This must be the tenth time."

"Thirteenth." She sighed. "I could spend all my nights with Kurt Russell." Elbowing Sara suggestively, she added, "If you get my meaning."

Sara nodded. "I believe I do. You're so naughty I blush."

Erma giggled her squeaky giggle. "If I were only seventy-five years younger, I'd give that Goldie person a run for her money." She sighed again. "But enough about my love life. What about you, you pretty little thing? I never see you with any of our local young men."

Sara's heart twisted, but she attempted to act nonchalant. "I'm awfully busy with my job—"

"Nonsense, child. Why, when I was your age I worked at a silk-stocking factory by day and checked hats at a speakeasy at night. I had a different beau with every snap of my fingers, and you're twice the beauty I was. I'll wager you have your own Kurt Russell tucked away somewhere. Is he in the service or something?"

Sara sidestepped the question, hoping her reply sounded lighthearted, though the old woman had hit upon the sorest spot in her life. "Erma," she said with a grin, "not everyone has your sex appeal."

Erma harrumphed. "Such a closemouthed thing you are." She frowned. "You never talk about yourself. But I've heard tell you met a very nice man when you traveled to Alaska."

Sara felt the blood drain from her face. Lynn must have told people about their visit to St. Catherine Island. And Andover was small enough that everybody knew everybody else's business. She fumbled with her purse, arranging it and rearranging it in her lap. "I—we met a lot of nice people up there," she hedged.

She could have added that Tag and Lynn had kept up a relationship via the mail. Sara knew, for instance, that Ransom had begun to date again. Lynn made it her solemn duty to read Tag's letters aloud, although Sara had no idea why she did. She supposed her sister simply wanted to share news of their faraway friends. Unfortunately what Lynn was really doing was pouring salt on the open wound in Sara's heart.

"But," Erma persisted, "I understand there was one very handsome, very wealthy man who—"

"Where did you hear that?" Sara interrupted, her voice sharper than she'd intended.

"Well, I was shopping for a Valentine gift for my great-granddaughter Felice. You know, the one who moved to Great Bend?" When Sara obediently nodded, Erma went on, "I stopped in the loud little boutique on Main called Teen Queen. Your sister helped me. Lovely child. She's a very good salesgirl."

"And a talkative one, I gather."

"Yes. She said she plans to make retail sales her career." Erma elbowed her riding companion again. "And do you know what else she said?"

"That she wants to have her lips sewn together for Valentine's Day?"

"Dear me, no!" Erma tittered appreciatively at Sara's quip. "No, what she said was that she met this handsome rich man who was very nice, and if she'd been a few years older she would've tried to make him fall in love with her and marry her."

Sara closed her eyes. The irrational daydream of marrying Ransom had hardly been out of her mind once in the past seven months, but with Erma's unexpected reminder, the desire rushed back with the intensity of a blow to the solar plexus.

"So," Erma went on, her voice full of curiosity, "I thought, since you *are* a few years older, you might have had a—" she giggled "—you know, a small *amour,* shall we say?" Sara was elbowed again as Erma added coyly, "My dear, we women of the world can speak frankly, can't we?"

Determined to put an end to this conversation, Sara turned toward her seat partner, her expression as pleasant as she could manage. "I'm afraid I'm not the woman of the world you are, Erma. There isn't anything to tell." She hoped her tone made it plain the subject was closed. She certainly had no intention of mentioning she was hopelessly in love with Ransom and, yes, they *had* shared a small *amour*—in the form of a few haunting kisses that had branded her lips and heart forever.

The bus stopped and several people got off. Sara looked at her watch. Nearly eight-thirty. She'd be home in ten minutes.

"Well, well..." Erma gave Sara yet another nudge in the ribs. "Goodbye, Kurt, hello, handsome stranger."

Confused, Sara glanced at Erma and saw she was gaping openly toward the front of the bus. As they began to move again, Erma grinned lecherously. "I wonder if that good-looking buck likes older women?"

Sara followed Erma's gaze and saw a powerfully built man deposit his fare and begin to walk down the aisle. His gray eyes met Sara's for a split second, and she almost fell to the floor of the bus in shock. She must have let out an audible gasp, for not only Erma, but several of the other passengers swiveled around to see what was wrong.

The man continued toward her, but seemed not to recognize her. Paralyzed in her seat, Sara could do little more than drink in his well-remembered physique. She knew her mind must be playing tricks on her, because there was no way on earth Ransom Shepard would be in Andover, Kansas, riding on the city bus. But this man, dressed in an impeccably tailored brown vicuña sport coat, black slacks, a black turtleneck and hand-finished loafers, looked exactly like Ransom.

Sara decided she must be having some sort of crazy hallucination. Her desire for him, mixed with fatigue from working double shifts, and possibly even toxic bus fumes, were making her see things that weren't real. Clearly there was a handsome man there, but it couldn't be Ransom.

The stranger sat down in the seat across the aisle and peered at his watch. Sara noticed the expensive timepiece glinting in the interior lights of the bus. She looked at his profile. It seemed to be the same ruggedly masculine face she'd fallen in love with on St. Catherine. But that was no doubt a vision caused by a raging fever she didn't know she had. She supposed that was a sign she was very ill indeed—too befuddled by sickness to even realize she was sick. Suddenly woozy, she rubbed a hand over her eyes, trying to dispel the fevered apparition.

Erma asked, "Are you feeling poorly, dear?"

"I—I must be coming down with something...."

"Excuse me," a resonant voice murmured.

Sara twisted around to find her face only inches from the man's. He'd leaned close. His cologne filled her nostrils and her body sang with remembrance. She swallowed hard, wondering whether she'd died and gone to heaven or whether Ransom Shepard, the man she loved with all her heart, was actually at her side.

"I'm new in town," he went on. "Does this bus go to McCloud Street?"

Sara could only nod dumbly.

"Why?" Erma interjected loudly. "Do you have family on McCloud?"

"Not yet," he said, shifting his gaze to the curious matron. "You see, there's a young woman who lives there. I plan to propose to her tonight." His eyes, compelling and magnetic, moved back to meet Sara's, and he smiled wryly at her surprise. "I don't deserve her, I know."

Erma prodded excitedly, "Who? Who's the young woman?"

He continued to look at Sara, his words no longer for anyone but her. "I let her leave me last summer, and I haven't been quite the same since. I've tried to forget her, dated women I didn't give a damn about, but my sleep and my business have suffered."

Sara watched, transfixed by the sincerity she saw in his face and heard in his voice. "That... that's a shame," she whispered.

He covered her hand with his, and she was aware of low murmuring from their fellow passengers as he said, "You see, I've had this problem with trust."

I know... she thought, but no sound came.

Ransom didn't seem to mind her silence. Smiling, he went on. "I've had a lot of time to think, and I've decided you're the person I need to help me through it."

Erma shouted triumphantly, "It's Sara! He's here to propose to Sara!" Obviously living a gossip's fondest dream, she threw her hands to her chest and wailed happily, "I may die!"

Ransom surveyed the ludicrous surroundings of his unorthodox proposal, then grinned. Pulling Sara to her feet, he took her into his arms and assured her huskily, "From Lynn's letters I know you started college, and I know you couldn't go this semester." His eyes glistened with love as he added softly, "We have colleges in Anchorage, Sara. And we need nurses there, too."

"I'm dying. I'm really dying!" squealed Erma. "Kiss her, you wonderful scoundrel. Kurt would!"

A frown began to cloud his features and he searched her pale face. "You haven't answered my question, Sara. Will you marry me?"

Her throat still blocked by emotion, wouldn't let her utter a sound.

Before her eyes, all pleasure seemed to leave his face. "Don't say no," he appealed softly. "I realize I was hard on you those last days, but I was afraid that if I touched you I wouldn't be able to let you go, and then I'd fall into the same trap I did with Jill. I didn't want to give anyone that much power over me again."

The hard-won honesty of his confession made his voice rough, and Sara's heart went out to him. "I—I do understand, Ransom," she managed.

Warmth radiated from him as he drew her closer and murmured quietly so only she could hear, "You're a caring person, Sara. I love you for that. When you left me, I found out that against my will I loved everything about you."

The devotion in his gaze would have staggered Sara if he hadn't been holding her snugly to him. "I love you, Ransom," she whispered solemnly. "I've loved you for so long...."

His eyes flashed with unguarded relief. "And?"

She blinked.

Hard male lips grazed her cheek as he reminded her, "You still haven't answered my question."

She flushed, suddenly self-conscious, but deliriously happy. "Yes, oh, yes. I'll marry you."

His expression became almost reverent. For an instant, he kissed her with his eyes. Then he lifted her face to his. Their lips met tenderly, and Sara's body tingled from the exquisite contact she'd craved for so long. Standing on tiptoe to enjoy the gentle persuasion of his mouth to its fullest, she curled her arms about his neck, savoring the taste of him.

Everyone on the bus began clapping and hooting. The delighted clamor broke through to Sara's consciousness and embarrassed, she pulled away from Ransom's arms.

"This is your stop, Sara," shouted the driver. "And have a happy wedding!"

"I knew it," declared Erma. "And you denied having a small *amour* up there in Alaska!"

Ransom's eyes contained a sensuous flame as he lifted the woman he loved into his arms and gently teased, "Why, Sara, did you deny our love?"

Heat rising in her cheeks, she snuggled against his chest. "I thought it was entirely one-sided," she admitted shyly.

With a hearty laugh, he turned to address the inquisitive old woman. "Madam, I'll have you know there was absolutely nothing small about our *amour,* and there never will be." Having said that, he swept Sara off the bus to the accompaniment of wolf whistles and boisterous cheering.

As the bus pulled away, Erma could be heard shouting, "Looking at you, mister, I can certainly see there'd be nothing *small* about it!"

Sara reached up and hugged Ransom. "I'll never hear the end of this."

Gracing the tip of her nose with a kiss, he countered, "You'll never hear the beginning. We're leaving for Anchorage tonight."

"We can't, not tonight. My things, Lynn..." she protested.

"I picked Lynn up from work early. She and your landlady have been packing for two hours. I've chartered a plane. My plan is to leave by eleven. So, we'll be tucked in bed at home by tomorrow morning."

The loving warmth of his smile echoed in his voice, and Sara could do nothing but smile back. But when the significance of his remark sank in, she had to say, "We won't be sleeping together—er, well, what I mean is, Lynn and Tag—"

"Unfortunately," he broke in, amusement glittering in his eyes, "The house in Anchorage does have several extra bedrooms. However, as soon as the paperwork is done and the vows are repeated, one guest bedroom will be vacated." He kissed her temple, whispering, "By the way, I like your hair."

Startled, she looked up at him. "It's not curly in Kansas."

"I don't care. I like it because it belongs to you."

"Oh, Ransom, I hope this blind devotion of yours doesn't wear off. It's wonderful!"

He sobered slightly and crushed her to him. "It's my biggest flaw," he muttered gruffly. "I tend to give my devotion blindly."

Tears welled in her eyes, and she moved slightly away so he could see the candor in her face. "Blind devotion isn't a flaw, Ransom. You're a good man who's been hurt badly. And I plan to earn your trust if it takes the rest of my life."

"I'll hold you to that," he vowed, "because I plan to love you for the rest of mine."

EPILOGUE

IT HAD BEEN TWO WEEKS since Ransom had gone to Andover to fetch Sara and her sister. During those two whirlwind weeks, the couple agreed that they wanted to be married on St. Catherine Island, where they'd met.

Sara was overwhelmed by the way the Pribilovians took her to their hearts as one of their own. And it tickled her to see Baby and Boo frolicking around in the village in their shaggy winter coats. Ransom had told her that one day they'd be released into the herd to mate, but they'd probably always come when called.

Today, Valentine's Day, every house in the village smelled of breads and festive foods prepared for the traditional wedding feast. Right now, however, on this snowy Bering Sea morning, all two hundred villagers were in the church or *barabera* which was half buried in the ground and built into the side of a hill. Jutting from its roof was the familiar white wooden steeple and green-tiled dome, visible over most of the island. Sara had been surprised to learn that the building, which seemed delightfully strange and old-fashioned to her, was actually a modern version of the Pribilovian underground church.

Sara hadn't seen Ransom today; she'd spent the morning with Lilly, Pat, Lynn and a few other island woman dressing in a traditional Pribilovian bridal costume and learning about the history of the islands. Lilly had explained that the Aleuts first came to the islands as forced labor for Russian fur traders. Gradually those two diverse cultures merged and evolved into the unique mix of high pomp and earthy simplicity the Pribilovians enjoy today.

Sara was fascinated by the wedding costume. The antique dress was well-suited to the harshness of Pribilovian weather. It was made of calf-length leather, lined with fur and decorated with colored beadlike rocks, seashells and a rainbow's hue of bird feathers. She found it to be heavy, yet felt feminine and somehow enchanted wearing a dress that had served Aleut brides for generations.

Her hair was tied back from her face by dyed and braided leather decorated with tinted shells and beads. One cheek had been painted with a small red flower. It was explained to her that the flower symbolized her coming "oneness" with another person—her husband. Sara smiled to herself. Oneness with Ransom. How wonderful to think of marriage that way.

Just before they left Lilly's home, the Aleut woman's mother proudly produced a flowing white wool cloak for Sara to wear on the chilly trek to the church. Sara felt like a princess from long ago and far away as she walked along, accompanied by Lilly, her mother and grandmother. Lilly had gladly offered her relatives as a surrogate family for Sara, and the women seemed happy to escort her through the still, twenty-degree morning to her husband-to-be.

A group of giggly girls, bundled up but clad in their best dresses, followed them through the two inches of fresh snow, visions of their own future weddings no doubt glittering brightly in their wide, dark eyes.

As the bridal procession neared the *barabera*, darkness had faded into a colorful late-morning dawn, and the sea and sky shimmered in shades of mauve, pink and rose. Sara looked about her, wondering if she had ever seen a lovelier daybreak, a lovelier place on earth.

The moment they reached the door, which was just beneath the roof, it magically opened. Obviously someone had been watching the women approach.

Isaac Dorfman stood in the doorway, all smiles, which startled Sara since Dan had offered to give her away. As Lilly lifted Sara's cloak from her shoulders, Sara said, "Why, Isaac, I didn't know you were here."

He gave her a brief hug and brushed her cheek and his lips. "Hey, I wouldn't miss this." With a wink he reminded her, "I'm responsible for getting you two together, remember?"

"I remember." Sara blushed, her face going hot in the cold air. "How can I ever repay you?"

"Name your kids after me."

Sara laughed. "Sure. How about Isaacetta and Dorfie?"

He chuckled, then nodded toward the open door. "Maybe we'd better get moving. There's a groom down there who's pretty anxious to see his bride, and I don't relish getting fired again today." Taking her hand, Isaac helped her down the ladder until her boots hit a packed-dirt floor covered with dried, fragrant tundra grasses.

Sara was struck by the spicy scent of incense and the rich, golden brightness of hundreds of flickering candles. The large room was completely full, though the place was hushed with the reverence of the ceremony.

As the rest of the entourage descended, Isaac silently placed Sara's hand within a warmer, larger one. She lifted her eyes to see Ransom standing beside her, regal and tall in his inherited wedding suit. His costume, too, was fashioned of tan leather and decorated with shells and stones. A rush of excitement went through her, making her shiver. His costume was of a past age, but his eyes flashed with an emotion that was older than even the spoken word, yet as recent as the day dawning above them. His love for her was strong and enduring, and that knowledge made Sara almost want to weep with joy.

With an encouraging smile that warmed her to her soul, he led her along the aisle toward the golden-robed priest. Lost in a fog of happiness, Sara was barely aware of what the priest murmured. As carved bone rings were exchanged amid prayers spoken in Aleut, Ransom bent close to explain the meaning—unity, oneness, a beginning.

Then, two wooden crowns, carved and encrusted with black diamonds, were brought forward by Lynn and Tag. Obviously proud to be included in the native ceremony, they presented the sparkling relics to the priest.

The holy man took the delicate crowns one at a time, blessed them, and then gently placed them, each in turn, on the bride and groom.

After that, bread was broken, and Ransom offered a piece to Sara. Seeing her confusion, he whispered, "Take a bite, my love. This is a symbol that I will care for you."

When she did, he said, "Now feed me."

She smiled shyly and held out her bread. When he took it between his lips, their eyes met. *Yes, I will love you, care for you, never hurt or betray you.* Sara made her soundless vow so passionately that a tear formed in her eye and slid down her cheek. Ransom saw it and Sara noticed that he had difficulty swallowing the bit of bread she'd given him.

Next, they shared a cup filled with mossberry juice, while a choir burst into a beautiful song. Though she didn't understand the words, Sara thought she'd never heard such an angelic gathering of voices.

Ransom reached across Sara and took her right hand, holding it toward the priest. She was startled when the holy man tied her wrist to Ransom's. As she looked toward her groom for guidance, he said, "We're to walk around the table."

Nodding, she walked with Ransom around the table that held the priest's accoutrements, along with a small plate filled with bits of breads and an empty cup. When they'd completed one full circle, Ransom prompted her forward again, whispering, "Three times, sweetheart."

Once this symbolic "dance of the trinity" was completed and their hands were untied, the priest removed their crowns with a final prayer.

The choir began again, and Sara glanced at her husband. He, too, was singing this ancient Aleut wedding song. He smiled at her and squeezed her hand, assuring her it was perfectly all right that she didn't know the song. As it drew to a close, Ransom leaned toward her and murmured, "A kiss isn't part of the ceremony, but if you'll recall, I'm only half Aleut."

Taking her in his arms, he kissed her tenderly. Ransom was now her husband. All the anger and sadness she had felt in his first kisses was gone and forgotten, like last winter's storms. She gloried in this kiss, growing weak with desire and need for him. Sighing softly, she clung to him, thrilled that they were spiritually one, with the physical oneness that marriage promised soon to come.

At last Ransom released her, but not before placing a loving kiss on her nose. Her heart fluttered wildly, and she could only stand there, staring longingly at the man she loved. His gaze as soft as a caress, he took his new bride by the hand and led her to the entryway.

As Sara ascended the ladder with her husband, she saw the two hundred upturned faces of the villagers, silent and smiling. She was awed to realize that many of those faces were streaked with tears of joy, perhaps recalling quiet memories of their own weddings.

When she and Ransom were finally standing alone in the brisk winter morning, Sara turned toward her grinning husband, her mind in a whirl. "What happens now?" she asked, breathless from the majesty of it all.

Placing her white cloak about her shoulders, he swept her into his arms. "There'll be a huge feast in the *barabera* as soon as the food arrives."

She sighed languidly, leaning her cheek against his. "I don't think I could eat a thing."

He chuckled and with one arm around her shoulders, began to walk toward his house. "That's probably just as well, my love, because we're not invited," he told her in a husky whisper. "You and I will be busy elsewhere."

She laughed with pure delight. "Oh, Ransom, your wedding customs are not only beautiful but wonderfully romantic. This has been the best Valentine's day I could ever imagine."

"Well, my sweet, sweet bride," he murmured, his lips teasing her earlobe, "the day has just begun...."

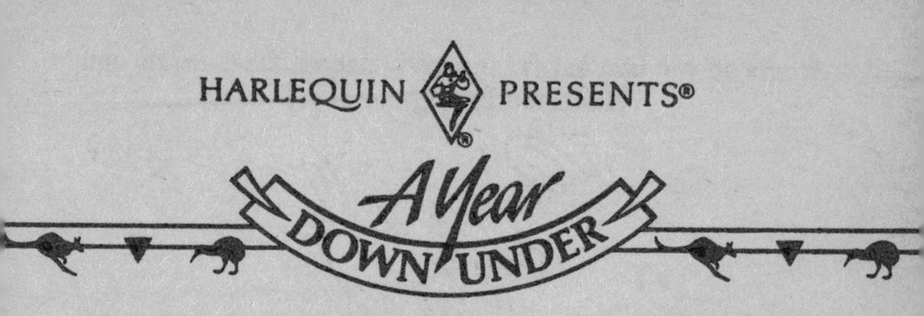
HARLEQUIN PRESENTS®
A Year
DOWN UNDER

Where do you find hot Texas nights, smooth Texas charm and dangerously sexy cowboys?

Wedding Bells—Texas Style!

Even a Boston blue blood needs a Texas education. Ranch owner J. T. McKinney is handsome, strong, opinionated and totally charming. And he is determined to marry beautiful Bostonian Cynthia Page. However, the couple soon discovers a Texas cattleman's idea of marriage differs greatly from a New England career woman's!

CRYSTAL CREEK reverberates with the exciting rhythm of Texas. Each story features the rugged individuals who live and love in the Lone Star State. And each one ends with the same invitation...

Y'ALL COME BACK...REAL SOON!

Don't miss ***DEEP IN THE HEART*** by Barbara Kaye. Available in March wherever Harlequin books are sold.

CC-1

Harlequin is proud to present our
best authors, their best books and
the best for your reading pleasure!
Throughout 1993, Harlequin will bring you
exciting books by some of the top names in
contemporary romance!
In February,
look for
Twist of Fate by
JAYNE ANN KRENTZ
Hannah Jessett had been content with her
quiet life. Suddenly she was the center of a
corporate battle with wealthy
entrepreneur Gideon Cage. Now Hannah
must choose between the fame and money
an inheritance has brought or a love that
may not be as it appears.
Don't miss TWIST OF FATE...
wherever Harlequin books are sold.
BOB1